THE PENGUIN CLASSICS

EDITORS:

*E. V. Rieu* (1944–64)
*Robert Baldick* (1964–72)
*Betty Radice*

There is very little information about Tibullus, apart from what can be gathered from his writings and the references to him by fellow writers. He was born round about 55 B.C., and his period of literary activity lasted little more than ten years. One or two Latin references lament his early death, which seems to have occurred shortly after Virgil's, 19–17 B.C. Tibullus came under the patronage of Marcus Valerius Messalla Corvinus, a trusted and powerful officer of the Emperor Augustus, and he appears to have gone with him on a campaign to Aquitania. Tibullus mentions in his work that they were left in Corfu by Messalla and his *cohors*, who went on to the eastern provinces; in circumstances such as these, which were often dangerous, Tibullus may well have developed his apparent hatred of war. There is extant a short biographical description of Tibullus which refers to him as young, handsome and chief among the elegy writers.

Philip Dunlop has been involved in translating since his schooldays and is at present teaching Classics at Manchester Grammar School, which, as he writes, 'is one of the leading schools engaged in preserving the best in traditional education in the classics and adapting it to modern conditions'.

GW00647818

*The Poems of*

# TIBULLUS

## WITH THE TIBULLAN COLLECTION

*Translated with an introduction by*

PHILIP DUNLOP

PENGUIN BOOKS

Penguin Books Ltd, Harmondsworth, Middlesex, England
Penguin Books Inc., 7110 Ambassador Road, Baltimore, Maryland 21207, U.S.A.
Penguin Books Australia Ltd, Ringwood, Victoria, Australia

—

This translation first published 1972

—

Copyright © Philip Dunlop, 1972

—

Made and printed in Great Britain
by Richard Clay (The Chaucer Press), Ltd,
Bungay, Suffolk
Set in Monotype Ehrhardt

# CONTENTS

# INTRODUCTION

*(i) Tibullus and the Tibullan Collection*

*The Poems of Tibullus* – so this book announces itself to the reader. Too many people today have regrettably not even heard of Tibullus, or at least find it hard to place him. A quick look at the Encyclopedia or a good literary history will do this much for us. Along with Propertius, Ovid, and the lost Gallus, Tibullus was one of the Latin elegiac poets who flourished in the reign of the emperor Augustus – the reign that also saw the birth of Virgil's *Aeneid* and most of the work of Horace. In such company it is not surprising that Tibullus gets a little lost – he is only *one* of the elegiac poets; who reads a poet because he is one of a group? We surely have a right to look for individuality and originality. The individual gifts of Propertius and Ovid have found their modern champions; Tibullus still waits for his. I hope that in the meantime this translation will go a little way towards making his poems better known and to establish his claim to be worth reading on his own account.

The full title of this book is *The Poems of Tibullus with the Tibullan Collection*. Who or what is the Tibullan collection? From the start we are faced with something of a literary mystery. The poems translated here have, like all Latin literature, come down to us in medieval MSS which derive ultimately from a Roman edition. These poems have reached us as a single collection in three books, with the name of one poet, Tibullus, at their head.[1] But the poems were not all written by Tibullus.

It is clear that ancient writers who discussed Tibullus' work

1. They will be referred to in the following pages and the glossary simply by the number of the book, the poem and the line – e.g. I.iii.55-6.

had only the first two books, the best and most consistent, in front of them; and there are other strong reasons for believing that Book Three is not, at least not entirely, the work of Tibullus. The first six poems of it, a clearly defined group, are written under the name of Lygdamus. This may be a *nom-de-plume*, but it is now generally agreed on grounds of style that the real author of these six poems, although at times he imitates Tibullus, is not Tibullus himself. The rest of the third book presents further difficulties, and may contain the work of as many as four other different poets. The 'Panegyric of Messalla', III.vii, is written in a different metre and technique, a different genre in fact, from the rest of the collection. Also it is a strong claimant for the title of worst surviving Latin poem. It reaches extremes of bathos and runs the gamut of fulsome flattery. It seems an inevitable conclusion that it was not written by a poet of Tibullus' calibre, though he too can be fulsome at times. It is perhaps most charitable to imagine it as someone's early work. After this come eleven short poems – III.viii–xviii. The last six of these are *very* short, and written in a clearly recognizable individual tone. They are presented as the work of Sulpicia, daughter of Servius. This Servius must be a member of the distinguished family of the Servii Sulpicii, who were related by marriage to the even more distinguished family of the Valerii Messallae. The head of this family is the 'Messalla' mentioned in III.xiv. This link between Sulpicia and Messalla makes her authorship of these poems quite credible, because Messalla and his household form a link that unites the whole collection, as we shall see. Three of the preceding five poems in this book, III.viii–xii, are also written in the person of Sulpicia, but this group, known as the 'Garland of Sulpicia', was evidently written by another poet around the events which Sulpicia had previously taken as the subject for her own poems. The stylish quality of these poems naturally suggests the idea that they are the work of Tibullus himself; but there are technical reasons for doubting this and placing their composition after Tibullus' death.

Finally, the collection includes two separate poems. The first, very much in Tibullus' manner, if rather flat in style, claims Tibullus as its author, but it could be the work of an imitator including his name for extra verisimilitude. The second is a short epigram; this again could be Tibullus' work – we have nothing, however, to compare it with. Stylistic analysis can prove very little in poems as short as these.

The poems of the third book, therefore, are by several different hands. Of these only Lygdamus and Sulpicia stand out as clear personalities to which we can put a name. The rest bear strong traces of Tibullus' influence, and some of them may even be his work. The common factor in all of them, along with the two authentic books of Tibullus, is the person of Messalla. It is a plausible suggestion that these poets formed some sort of literary circle centred on Messalla's household. Mutual discussion and comparison of work in progress was an important part of Roman literary activity at all levels; amateurs might never take things any further, and this was perhaps also true of cultured women, who would hardly be encouraged to give public recitations – now rapidly becoming the norm as the first step in bringing one's work before the public at large. We have no evidence that any of these poets except Tibullus were ever separately published; apart from anything else, their *œuvre*, as we know it, would have been simply too small. A rich patron with literary interests of his own, such as Messalla, who could encourage and support his protégés would make an ideal centre for such a group. One imagines Tibullus, with one or both of his books already published, as the young lion of the circle, admired and imitated by the others.

But granted that the poems we have are the work of such a group, it is still something of a mystery how they got collected together and handed down to us in the form in which we possess them. As I have suggested, Tibullus' own works were certainly published and well known in his own lifetime, and presumably private copies of the other poems had been made. Probably at some stage someone connected with Messalla or his circle decided to make a collection of the best work of the group, including Tibullus' already published work. It could be purely accidental that this copy of Tibullus alone survived to become the ancestor of our modern editions. An alternative possibility is that the lesser poems were added to Books I and II because a large proportion of them, at least, are really the works of Tibullus; or that a later Roman editor came across them and mistakenly took them to be Tibullus' work. At all events poems such as these which give us a kind of cross-section of the poetry of the age are a valuable possession; in fact we would be very loath to lose Sulpicia's small masterpieces and their charming companion-pieces.

## (ii) The Patronage of Messalla

Messalla himself, the patron of Tibullus and the poets of Book Three, was a remarkable man. His full name, Marcus Valerius Messalla Corvinus, reveals him as a member of a distinguished and high-ranking Roman family. After the murder of Julius Caesar in 44 B.C., true to his class, he joined the outlawed republicans, Brutus and Cassius, and at the age of twenty-two commanded the right wing of their army at the battle of Philippi in 42 B.C. Perhaps he was merely too young to allow his career to be extinguished along with the republican cause; perhaps he foresaw the future course of Roman politics; at any rate, after the defeat of Philippi he transferred his allegiance to the victor, Mark Antony. Julius Caesar's great-nephew, the young Caesar, had performed most unpromisingly at the battle, and Antony would have seemed the man in the best position to restore some stability to the state. But Antony soon outraged Roman opinion by his political alliance with Cleopatra, and his treatment of his wife, the young Caesar's sister Octavia. Messalla was one of the very first men of family and rank to align himself with the young Caesar (although it was Caesar, according to popular story, who had previously added his name to the list of those proscribed in 43 B.C.). For this the future emperor was greatly in his debt, and political indebtedness was not borne lightly by Roman nobles. Messalla became one of his most trusted lieutenants in the war with Sextus Pompeius in 36 B.C.; against the tribes of Yugoslavia in 35-34 B.C. (it is these campaigns and Messalla's part in them that the Panegyric – III.vii.106 ff. – so lovingly refers to); against the Alpine Salassi in 33 B.C.; and then as fellow consul with Caesar in 31 B.C. at the battle of Actium, where Antony was decisively defeated. Some time later, in the decade 30-20 B.C., the tribes of south-west Gaul rebelled. Messalla was chosen to deal with them, and for his success in this campaign he received the honour of a Triumph (see I.vii). Soon after he was sent out to the provinces in the east to settle various problems that had arisen. Whether Messalla was among those who had expected Caesar to restore the republican constitution when the campaigns were over and the provinces settled, we do not know. It is easy for us with hindsight to see the political settlement of 27 B.C. as the foundation of the empire, but at the time it was presented as a return to constitutional government. At any rate, when Messalla was appointed in 26 B.C. to the freshly created post of *Praefectus Urbis*, he resigned after a few days in office. Whether he thought the authority vested in the post 'undemocratic' (Latin *incivilem*) or merely claimed incompetence, as our sources variously tell us, we shall never know. In later times such a course would have seemed a dangerous act of independence. Certainly Messalla was no creature of the new emperor's (henceforward known as Augustus) as so many of the remodelled senate were; but neither was he a hotheaded rebel. His action is perhaps just that of a self-confident man born to power and influence who could take Augustus' 'return to constitutionalism' at its face-value. He continued to serve Augustus with undiminished loyalty. He reconstructed the *Via Latina* so efficiently that a hundred years later it was still a byword for durability (see I.vii.57 ff.). In 11 B.C. he became the first *curator aquarum* in charge of Rome's aqueducts. His son Messalinus, whose election as *quindecimvir* in charge of the Sibylline books is celebrated in II.v, embarked on an equally loyal and almost equally distinguished career. It is in his last recorded action that we may feel that Messalla finally went too far and betrayed his aristocratic heritage. In 2 B.C., he was the man who proposed in the senate that Augustus be given the flattering title of *Pater Patriae* – 'Father of the Fatherland'. But all in all it was a splendid life.

Messalla's literary patronage is very much of a piece with his career in public life. One of the most remarkable things about him is that at a time when Augustus was devoting a certain amount of energy to fostering and controlling the best literary talent of the day, Messalla should have been able to extend patronage of his own. Virgil, Horace and Propertius were all taken up by Augustus' friend and adviser Maecenas, and however sincerely Virgil, for example, may have wished to glorify the new age of Augustus on his own account, it is evident that there was a certain amount of pressure on these writers to write in conformity with the particular spirit of the age which Augustus wished to nurture. Ovid, independent of imperial patronage, was subsequently banished, at least partly for the matter of his poetry, which conflicted with Augustus' aims for the moral regeneration of Rome. Propertius felt threatened for similar reasons. Yet all this was while the poets patronized by Messalla were celebrating not Augustus' military exploits, but Messalla's; not the virtues of Augustus' son-in-law Marcellus, but those of Messalla's son Messalinus. Tibullus furthermore discussed the techniques of love in such a way that Ovid could later point to his work and ask why, if he himself had been exiled for his *Amores* and *Ars Amatoria*, Tibullus had gone unpunished.[2] Of course Tibullus' poetry is never consistently and blatantly amoral in mood, as Ovid's is, and Ovid was banished long after Tibullus' death when Augustus had grown much more autocratic; but we might still wonder how Tibullus managed to evade similar pressures. Why was he not co-opted for what we might call the court literary circle? Did Maecenas approach him, as he had approached Virgil, Horace and Propertius, only to be met with a firm and independent-spirited refusal? We can put such questions in perspective by taking in the wider view of the whole Roman institution of patronage. The Roman concept of patronage was something much broader than our idea of artistic patronage. The relationship of *patronus* and *cliens* pervaded politics, the law, and every level of private life, shading off imperceptibly into *amicitia* – 'friendship' – itself almost an official status in the political world. Virgil had first approached Augustus to request the return of his father's estates, confiscated during the civil wars. When Augustus, probably through Maecenas, acceded to this request, he was laying the foundations of a patron's *tutela* – 'protection' – in a much broader way than if he had merely been promising to keep Virgil in pocket until his literary work was completed. Similarly we must imagine Tibullus (who perhaps did not need much in the way of material support) and some of the other poets of our collection not merely as the receivers of literary encouragement from Messalla, but as his *clientes* or *amici* in the broader sense. This relationship may have been initiated in a number of ways – patronage could be heredi-

2. Ovid: *Tristia*, II.447–64.

tary, for example, or simply geographical. Otherwise a man of Messalla's literary interests might take the initiative in attaching promising young writers to himself; conversely an ambitious young man in any field might offer his services or friendship to the kind of man who would appreciate his talents. Given this relationship already existing between Tibullus and Messalla, we can see that Tibullus was simply not in the necessary unattached state for any other patron to extend his patronage to him. Ministers of propaganda can command universal conformity (or silence), but a poet only needs one patron; and Maecenas was not Augustus' minister of propaganda, however helpful it may be to think of him sometimes in this light. Nor was Messalla being dangerously independent in encouraging his client poets to write in the way they did at such a time. He was an unusual man – one of the few remaining men of rank and 'nobility' to have survived the civil wars. The way in which he combined a political career not only with the useful pursuit of oratory, but with his private literary interests too – poetry, philosophy, and linguistics – reminds us of the great men of the republic – Cato, Scipio Aemilianus, even Julius Caesar. It was with the same aristocratic confidence that Messalla protected and encouraged poets (not only those of his immediate circle; Ovid in his youth was encouraged by Messalla to publish). His protégés were not disloyal citizens; neither were they required to go out of their way to touch on matters irrelevant to their art; he himself, as their patron, and as such an integral part of their lives, could never be an irrelevant subject. For Messalla and his circle it was in many ways a happy period. Stability and peace had been restored to Rome by Augustus, and yet they could continue to live as if the empire had not yet come into being. The serenity of their work is something that could not perhaps have been found in the troubled times of the republic, and perhaps could never exist again under autocracy.

Of the lives of the poets of Messalla's circle we know virtually nothing. Sulpicia identifies herself as Messalla's niece by marriage, and it sounds from her poetry (see III.xiv) as if he were her legal guardian; this would explain her living in his house and how she came to be a member of the circle. The episodes of her love-affair are probably based on her real experience. The relationship of art to life in Roman poetry is a complex one, but as far as we can tell the situations this type of poetry presents are usually based on actual experience, and the loved ones are drawn from real people whose identities are merely disguised by pseudonyms. Cerinthus is very likely the pseudonym of a real young man. Some have thought he is the Cornutus of Tibullus II.ii and iii, though of course he does not have to be anyone we already know about. If Sulpicia's real-life love-affair was condoned by Messalla we can guess that at any rate Cerinthus was in the normal respects eligible for a girl from such a well-connected family.

Lygdamus' name is a real puzzle. Latin poets do not usually use pseudonyms for *themselves*. But if Lygdamus is his real name, he sounds like a Greek freedman. There is nothing intrinsically unlikely in this. Latin literature as we know it owed a great deal to non-Roman freedmen living in the households of cultured patrons. Some have professed to see evidence in Lygdamus' unidiomatic Latin. But a clever Greek could probably handle literary Latin just as well as, for example, Joseph Conrad handled English. Nor do we suspect every author who shows an occasional clumsiness of style of having a foreign origin. In fact this poet uses the phrase 'our ancestors' when describing an essentially Roman custom (III.i), and talks as if he owned an independent dinner-table (III.vi). He is at least adopting the literary *persona* of a well-off Roman. He gives us one hard biographical fact when he says (III.v.18) that he was born in 'the year coincident fate felled both consuls together'. Ovid uses the same historical reference to date his own birth.[3] Both poets are referring to 43 B.C., when the two consuls, Hirtius and Pansa, were both mortally wounded at the battle of Mutina.

For the other poets we have not even a name, let alone a biography. The events in Messalla's career referred to in the Panegyric all occurred before 33 B.C., so that this poem is very likely one of the earliest in the collection (but perhaps not early enough to be a juvenile effusion of Tibullus'). Its excessive flattery might indicate that its author was particularly indebted to the patronage of Messalla, but this is only guessing. If the 'Garland of Sulpicia' is not by Tibullus, it probably dates from the period just after his death, when Lygdamus was also writing; both poets seem to owe a clear debt to the work of Propertius, who died in 16 B.C., and perhaps also, in the case of the 'Garland', to the early work of Ovid.

## (iii) *Life of Tibullus*

We do have a little more information about Tibullus himself, but only a very little. The poems of Book I reflect the historical facts of Messalla's Aquitanian campaigns (I.vii), his visit to the Eastern provinces (I.iii and vii), and the rebuilding of the *Via Latina* (I.vii). The book could have been published, therefore, any time after about 27 B.C. – the exact date of the road-repairs is not known. The second book contains fewer chronological clues. We do not know the exact date of Messalinus' appointment as *quindecimvir sacris faciundis*, the event celebrated in II.v, but he was still in office in 17 B.C., and was perhaps appointed not many years before this. Tibullus' death can be placed sometime after the autumn of 19 B.C. Domitius Marsus, a contemporary writer of epigrams, wrote of it thus:

3. Ovid: *Tristia*, IV.x.6.

Death is unfair and has sent you too to be Virgil's companion,
  Sent you while still in your prime down to Elysian fields,
So no man should survive to bemoan sweet love with his couplets,
  Nor in the high bold strain sing of the battles of kings.

The point of the epigram seems to be that Tibullus died not
long after Virgil, who died on the 20th September 19 B.C. It is
difficult to judge how far the two deaths could have been separa-
ted and still allowed the epigram its point. Both Tibullus' II.v,
and a lament for his death written by Ovid,[4] echo in some res-
pects the content and language of Virgil's *Aeneid*, which was
not actually published until 18 or 17 B.C., but could probably
have been heard at least in part at private readings well before
this. A little later Ovid also wrote[5] of 'The Greedy Fates',
which denied time to his friendship with Tibullus and confirms
the suggestion in the epigram that Tibullus died early. In the
following couplet Ovid places him after Gallus (born 65 B.C.) and
before Propertius and himself in the chronological sequence of
Roman elegiac poets. All told, the picture we get is of a man
whose working life began in the twenties B.C., perhaps after
returning from abroad with Messalla, and which lasted little
more than about ten years; we can tentatively place his date of
birth around 55 B.C.

To this extent our information is fairly objectively based. There
are other sources which need more care in their interpretation.
At the end of the edition of Tibullus which we have inherited
stands the epigram of Domitius Marsus which I have just
quoted, and together with it a short biographical note:

Albius Tibullus, a Roman knight, notable for his looks and con-
spicuous for his exquisite grooming, was particularly attached to
Corvinus Messalla, and as a member of Messalla's mess in the Aqui-
tanian war was presented with military decorations. In the judgement

4. Ovid: *Amores*, III.ix.    5. Ovid: *Tristia*, IV.ix.51–2.

of many he holds the chief place among the writers of elegy. His amatory epistles also, though brief, are totally rewarding. He died a young man as the above epigram indicates.

Unfortunately every piece of information in this note is probably reconstructed from other literary sources, including Tibullus' own poetry – sources we are independently familiar with and might well interpret differently. It is even probable that the 'amatory epistles' referred to are not in fact a lost and otherwise unknown work of Tibullus' but simply the shorter poems of Book III, some of which are certainly epistolary in form. The writer's method is clearly illustrated when he refers us to the Domitius Marsus epigram as his authority for Tibullus' early death. In fact the wording of the epigram is imprecise, and we would not rely on it as evidence without the testimony of Ovid to back it up. The word used is *iuvenis*, which can refer to almost any age up to fifty! The writer also tells us that in many people's opinion Tibullus held the first place among writers of elegiac poetry. The statement could simply be based on the remarks of Quintilian in his well-known summary of Latin literature.[6] Quintilian lists the four main writers of Latin elegy – Gallus, Tibullus, Propertius and Ovid – with a short comment on each. It could be judged from these comments that although there were some who rated Propertius higher, respectable opinion preferred Tibullus (Gallus being too harsh, and Ovid too frivolous). So far, however, our biographical note is uncontroversial. But we are also told that Tibullus' family name was Albius, that he was of equestrian status, well-groomed, and handsome. These remarks almost certainly derive from one of two poems by Horace,[7] which he addressed to an elegiac poet called Albius. Horace's Albius may well indeed be Tibullus; Romans could be

6. Quintilian: *Institutio Oratoria*, X.i.93.
7. Horace: *Epistles*, I.iv and *Odes*, I.xxxiii.

addressed by either their family name or their *cognomen*, and Horace's portrait fits well in other respects, but if our writer is basing his statement of Tibullus' wealth (and by inference his equestrian status) on Horace's fourth Epistle, Horace's words are (*Epistles*, I.iv):

You were never mere body without a heart: the gods gave you beauty,
The gods gave you wealth and the art of enjoying it.

Now Tibullus himself talks of his poverty (I.i.5). We have a fine example here of the relativity of this kind of literary evidence. On the one hand Horace is pointing in this poem to Albius' fitness to lead a wise and worth-while life on the Epicurean model, which principally involves absence of hardship – indeed he defines this further a few lines later with the phrase 'a nice diet, and a purse that doesn't get empty': on the other hand Tibullus gives a picture of a modest and retired life in the country which is meant to contrast with that of the greedy militarist; he is also comparing his present resources with the perhaps even more substantial means of his ancestors. In the other poem to Albius (*Odes*, I.xxxiii) Horace gives a teasing impression of his friend 'chanting his mournful elegiacs' and thinking of 'the harsh Glycera'. It would be a great mistake to assume that Glycera is the pseudonym of a girl who was to be the inspiration of a third book of Tibullan elegies, or had been the subject of unpublished juvenilia. Horace is perhaps merely representing his friend in a typical pose – basically a literary pose; the name Glycera is derived from the Greek for 'sweet' and was probably selected with its epithet for a touch of irony. We would be on much surer ground looking at the first two lines of the Epistle if we want concrete information. Horace writes to Albius as resident in the region around Pedum. He may have been just visiting, or on holiday, but at any rate we must accept this kind of detail as being credible of the real Albius. If Albius really is Tibullus, Pedum, a small town in Latium near Rome, might even be his home. If so, Tibullus can claim to have been more nearly a Roman than most Latin poets.

The last piece of information that the anonymous life gives us is that Tibullus was a member of Messalla's mess during the Aquitanian campaigns and received military decorations. Unless we believe the writer had access to independent sources, this must be a conclusion drawn from Tibullus' own poem (I.vii) which refers to these campaigns. The poem begins by discussing Messalla's triumph, and then Tibullus says 'I shared in these honours', and calls to witness the rivers and mountains of the area. The remark is vague enough. It is initially much more probable that he went to Aquitania, if at all, as a member of Messalla's *cohors* – the semi-official body of *clientes* and *amici* who followed Roman generals to their campaigns. In I.iii he actually talks of being left behind by Messalla and his *cohors* at Corfu on their way to the eastern provinces. Caesar gives us a vivid picture of the terrors experienced by such a group when his army marched against the Germans in 58 B.C., and they found themselves in real danger.[8] In circumstances like these Tibullus could well have developed the horror of war which he displays frequently in his poems, and, if he had shared in the risks, could perhaps also consider himself to have shared in the 'honours' of the expedition; but I doubt if he could have qualified for military decorations.

There is little else of Tibullus' life that we ourselves can even tentatively reconstruct from the evidence of his poems. In general we can say that the events which are represented in them are very likely based on experience (e.g. his falling sick in Corfu in I.iii), and that the *persona* progressively created in the sixteen different poems bears some relation to Tibullus' historical self. Horace remonstrating with Albius not to be so dismal and

8. Caesar: *De Bello Gallico*, I.xxxix.

preoccupied with his love-affairs must bear the same sort of indirect witness to his personality. Friends are mentioned in several poems – Cornutus in II.ii and iii, and Macer in II.vi. We know nothing of Cornutus; there seems no positive reason to believe that he is the Cerinthus of Sulpicia's poems, as was once suggested, just as it is unlikely that Tibullus wrote 'The Garland of Sulpicia' – the chronology does not fit. Macer is probably the contemporary poet Aemilius Macer, much admired in his day. Tibullus was of course acquainted with a much wider circle of literary friends than those he met in Messalla's house. Both Horace and Ovid were members of this wider circle. Another probably was Valgius Rufus, mentioned in the Panegyric – III.vii.179–80. The lines suggest that Valgius was also a client of Messalla's, though the fact that he was a close friend of Horace's may equally well mean that he was a protégé of Maecenas. Tibullus also refers in I.iv to a man named Titius. This may not be intended as a real-life reference, but if there was a Titius who was a friend of Tibullus he may well be the Titius described by Horace as a poet 'shortly to arrive on Roman lips'.[9]

Finally we come to those we may call the protagonists in the drama – Delia and Nemesis (and Lygdamus' Neaera), and the minor roles, Marathus and Pholoe. These people no doubt existed in the lives of their poets, as did Catullus' Lesbia and Propertius' Cynthia. The names are probably disguises. We are actually told by one writer,[10] for what it is worth, that Delia's real name was Plania. I shall be saying quite a lot later about the position in Roman society of such people, at any rate as it is represented in the poems. But we must avoid the temptation to try to construct a consistent biographical framework round the poems that concern them. Those who have tried have usually failed. Latin elegiac poetry was never intended to be autobiography in verse. Perhaps it is now time to consider what it was

9. Horace: *Epistles*, I.iii.9.       10. Apuleius: *Apologia*, X.

intended to be, and to take a look at some of the history and conventions of the genre.

## (iv) Elegiac Poetry as a Genre

In Tibullus' time elegiac poetry constituted a specific genre of its own. Whatever the modern connotations of the word 'elegiac', the description, when applied to Greek and Latin literature simply specifies poetry written in elegiac couplets – i.e. pairs of lines, each pair consisting of a hexameter and a pentameter – a six-foot and a five-foot line – which are made up metrically of a mixture of dactyls and spondees. To a certain extent genre is always tied up with metre. To take an extreme example, it would be virtually impossible today to write a serious poem in the metre of a limerick. Likewise in classical times the plain hexameter was indissociably linked with epic and the grander poetic themes (though it could also stoop to take in pastoral). The elegiac couplet was at best a *lighter* metre, often considered *playful*, though perhaps always grander in large numbers than, for example, Catullus' hendecasyllables and short epigrams, which he describes as 'trifles'; on the other hand, whatever its origins, by the Roman period it lacked the musical associations of the so-called 'lyric' metres, such as those used by Horace. However, in Greek literature the elegiac couplet was not used exclusively for any one kind of style or subject. It could handle moral teaching, martial encouragement, epitaph, epigram, reflective and personal poetry all with equal success. Even in Greek times its actual name was particularly associated with the idea of threnody, or at least a melancholy kind of poetry, and attempts were made to explain its name in terms of the Greek phrase *ĕ ĕ legein* – 'to cry woe'. But certainly the earliest surviving Greek elegists are among the least mournful and melancholic of all.

Perhaps the only thing that does link the Greek elegists from the seventh century B.C. right down to the poets of third-century Alexandria is a kind of basic mood or tone, or perhaps a nexus of moods and tones, which derive from the nature of the metre itself.

The couplet begins with a firm hexameter, whose rhythm carries through unbroken to the end of the line. This is followed by the briefer pentameter, with its prominent break in the rhythm, creating two equal half-lines. The pentameter is more predominantly dactylic, its second half-line in Augustan elegy entirely so. The couplet usually forms a complete unit of sense, and the individual lines very often do so. Antithesis is thus a natural mode of expression, with one line being set against the other. It is easy to see how the couplet became the favoured vehicle for epigram. But the metre also encourages a certain tone – a tone which is personal, poignant and often wry. The comparatively short phrases give an impression that life is best dealt with in brief, or at least that rhetoric and bombast are to be set aside. The rhythm encourages an elegance and a verbal compression that in the hands of the best poets give rise to phrases of haunting, lapidary beauty. At the same time the texture of continuous successive couplets can reflect the natural flow of the poet's thought and avoid the composed artificiality of the lyric metres.

The metre first became popular in Rome in the first half of the first century B.C. This was an exciting period for Roman poetry. The poets of the day were discovering and quarrying the riches of Greek literature, particularly the work of the Alexandrian period. Alexandria, with its famous library, had become the centre of the Greek literary world in the third and second centuries B.C. A new style in poetry had developed – learned, often precious, and setting much more store by novelty and originality. At best it manifested a new awareness of the individual and the personal.

Countless epigrams played on the joys and sorrows of humble individuals. Narrative poetry explored with an acute perception the feelings of its characters. Words, often unusual and recondite, were chosen and placed with great artistry. Echoes of the past, frequently in the form of mythological allusions, were woven into the texture, adding richness and distance. The best Latin poets, notably Catullus, studied the Alexandrians with enthusiasm, and fused much of their influence into their individual style; the second-rate poets seem to have written verse more arid and pedantic than any of their models. And at some time between the age of Catullus and the age of Augustus, somehow, out of the melting-pot of the Roman, classical Greek, and Alexandrian heritage, the new genre of Latin elegiac poetry emerged. For one element in this new genre Catullus himself was primarily responsible. This element is the new subjective approach to love and its attendant passions. The psychology of love had been widely explored by Greek writers, even in the classical period. Alexandrian epigrammatists had ironically commented on the vicissitudes of love as it affected them or their friends. Mimnermus and Sappho, to name but two of the older Greek poets, had said almost all there is to say about the joy and the pain of love. Certain Greek poets whose works have not survived have been thought by some to have actually written a series of poems round their own love for a particular mistress. But it seems from surviving fragments and commentaries that at most these poems amounted to little more than catalogues and narratives of comparable love-affairs from history and mythology. Catullus is the first to explore consistently the subjective experience of a love-affair – in the series of elegiacs and hendecasyllables written round his feelings for the infamous Clodia. The time was probably made the more ripe for this by the publication of an equally revolutionary poet, Lucretius, who in his scientific and philosophical poem on the make-up of the universe had recently discussed the pathology of passion. Part of Catullus' technique in recreating the feelings of the lover is to suggest this physical correlative to the emotions. Most of Catullus' elegiacs are short epigrams in form, but in one or two poems he combines the sharp reaction and sting of the epigram with a more reflective and discursive vein; these poems are really the first creations in the new genre.

Although these poems of Catullus were written in an erotic context, we must not think that elegiac poetry is confined to love-poetry. Every poem in Tibullus' attested work contains some reference to his love; but no one could describe, say, the poem on Messalla's triumph (I.vii) or the description of the country festival (II.i) as being primarily love-poetry. Propertius and Ovid were to stray even further from themes of love in their elegiacs without necessarily exceeding the genre. Propertius and Ovid sometimes wrote as if their work was entirely erotic, especially in their earlier poems. Indeed the title of one of Ovid's works is simply *Amores* – 'Loves'. They also followed the convention that the poems they are writing are to be thought of as real communications to their mistresses, designed to win her over. Ovid in particular suggests that these are the circumstances in which love-poetry has always been written, and cites lists of earlier poets, right back to Mimnermus (seventh century B.C.), adding sometimes the names of the mistresses who both inspired them and received their outpourings. Both Propertius and Ovid mention particularly among those to whom they owe a debt, the Alexandrian poets Philitas and Callimachus. This has given rise to the idea that there was already in existence a genre of 'erotic elegy', a characteristic mark of which was the production of books or groups of books centred like Propertius' first book (known as 'Cynthia Monobiblos') on the poet's love for a single female. But as I have already said, such fragments as survive of these poets do not suggest that if such a tradition existed it could have supplied much of a model for the poems the Latin elegists actually wrote. The poets Ovid names form a multifarious list, and the most striking references in Propertius to Philitas and Callimachus occur in poems where he seems to be moving away from simple love-elegy and to be preoccupied with style as much as with form. I shall return to the convention that Ovid is exploiting, but it must be recognized as a convention.

In fact it is abundantly clear that in all its details Latin elegy owes an immeasurable amount to Greek poetry and its themes and conventions. Many of the situations presented (e.g., the lover outside his mistress' locked door), and the rhetorical tropes employed (e.g., the lists of precedents, and indeed lists of all kinds, like the list of those condemned in the underworld in Tibullus I.iii) are suggested by Greek originals, particularly from the Alexandrian period. So little Alexandrian poetry has survived that we shall probably never know the precise extent of these influences. But Latin elegy remains basically different in character from anything in Greek literature. Nothing has survived which runs counter to this. What distinguishes Latin elegy is the new subjectivism, which surely owes most to Catullus and his successors. I do not mean by this that the Latin elegists are always talking exclusively about themselves and their emotions. Some of Tibullus' poems, for example, are mainly about other people. But it is Tibullus' awareness of Cornutus' marriage in II.ii, and his sharing in the experience of Messalinus' election in II.v, that give the poems the character they have. The 'Garland of Sulpicia' (III.viii–xii) is also written completely about a love affair in which the poet is not directly involved. But I think these poems arise out of the already existing conventions of Latin elegy. For all the influence of Greek lyric poetry these conventions suggest, the second half of III.ix could surely not have been written until after the 'Catullan revolution'. If, as seems likely, they were written after about 20 B.C. then they come in a period when simple subjective love-elegy was already beginning to seem a little outmoded, and both Ovid and Propertius were moving on to new subjects for their elegies. Of the later works of these two we can perhaps say that the subjective element as such has ceased to be important; what counts is that they are writing in the elegiac form with the responses which were developed through subjective love-elegy.

This type of poetry, then, is what we mean when we speak of Latin elegy. It is built up on many of the same tones and moods that I claimed were the common factor in Greek elegy and arose out of the nature of the metre. The metre was in fact restricted in its flexibility by the poets of Augustus' reign in two important respects. First, the couplet is now almost always an enclosed unit of sense, and the individual lines much more often so than in Greek. Secondly the pentameter was required to end with a completely dactylic second half-line, rounded off with a dissyllable. This tripping, almost anti-climactic rhythm fosters a certain kind of elegance and witty understatement (much exploited by Ovid). But as before, the metre serves as the vehicle for the poignant, the graceful, and the expression of sensibility. Ovid describes himself as *tenerorum lusor amorum* – the poet who made play with *tender* loves. He uses the word elsewhere; the poets in one of his lists of erotic predecessors are described as *teneros poetas*. The word is significantly one of Tibullus' favourite epithets for all kinds of things. The elegiac poet, in other words, is one who is alive to what is *tener*, or *mollis* (soft), a favourite word of Propertius'. Conversely the poet eschews all that is *durus* (see Lygdamus III.ii.1ff.). These are conclusions we can draw from the poetry itself. But the poets also occasionally give us hints of their own view of their role as elegiac poets. I was describing above the convention whereby the poet's works are thought of not merely as being inspired by his loved one (see II.v.111), and perhaps giving fame to her (e.g., III.iv.57), but

also as being used to win her over (cf.II.iv.19). The idea appears
in its most commonplace form in Lygdamus (III.i.7) – 'Beauti-
ful girls are caught by rhyme.' Ovid's lists of erotic poets often
occur in contexts where he is recommending the kind of general
reading a lover should introduce to his beloved. Likewise Pro-
pertius advises a friend (III.ix), who has fallen in love to give up
writing serious poetry and take up elegy:

In love the metre of Mimnermus has more power than Homer.

A similar idea that seems first to occur in Tibullus (I.iv)
is that the poet is in some way a *teacher* of love, and his love-
affair a *textbook* to others (I.vi.86). We should certainly recog-
nize all these ideas as basically poetic conventions, but the
conventions reflect a very real situation. In one poem, talking of
his art, Propertius prays that his works may find acceptance
among the poems of Callimachus and Philitas; he then con-
tinues:

May these writings of mine set the young men and the girls on fire:
  Let them acclaim me as a god and bring me sacrifice.

Propertius really hoped to have the kind of effect on his public
that, for example, the English romantic poets had. He wanted not
merely to please the public with his poetic vision, but, helped by
the style and technique of Callimachus and Philitas, to fire his
readers with his own sensibility and alter their life-style with it.
He wants his books to be on every young person's bedside stool
(see Propertius: III.xix.20). Indeed it is clear that in this period
there must have been a new, younger, and more liberal public for
poetry growing up – I shall mention this again later. Now Tibul-
lus has none of Propertius' extravagant ambition, and the ideas
of fiery reaction or divine status are not ones we quickly associate
with him, yet this couplet of Propertius' gives us some idea of
the relationship aimed at by the Latin elegiac poets between

28

themselves and their readers. Ultimately it is the art and the personal sensibility, not the content that makes the genre. Hence the predominance, but not the exclusive place of love in these poets' subject matter; hence also their ability, especially noticeable in Tibullus, to pass from love to other themes and back again with no sense of a rude transition.

## (v) The Social Background

Tibullus is a very important figure in the history of this genre, because, apart from Catullus, his first book is the earliest complete example of it to survive. Many of the conventions and commonplaces that recur in Propertius and Ovid and seem to us an indissociable part of elegiac poetry may have been originated by Tibullus. Ovid, it is true, recognizes three predecessors in the genre – Propertius, Tibullus, and before them Gallus. Unfortunately we have almost no direct knowledge of Gallus' work. There is some evidence to suggest there was a strong pastoral element in it; Gallus played on the theme of love in the countryside, that is to say, and perhaps also the idea of the lover pursuing the beloved through trials and misfortunes. Tibullus' work also shows this pastoral strain in the pictures he presents of idyllic life with Delia on his farm. But if the pastoral element was Gallus' main contribution to the tradition of elegiac poetry, it may well be that the more urban and social elements in the Tibullan background, which Propertius and Ovid so brilliantly developed, were an original contribution to the tradition. Certainly Ovid suggests that Tibullus was the man who originated in elegy the convention of the poet as the teacher of the art of love, love in this context being love in a sophisticated and more or less amoral urban society. Tibullus may also be to a large extent responsible for introducing the actual details of life in the

Roman *demi-monde* which quickly became the accepted stage-machinery of elegiac – the houses with watchdogs, night-watchmen and creaking doors, the keepers and go-betweens, the drinking parties and the other lovers passing the door, the secret signs and rendezvous. Some of this apparatus may be borrowed from Greek poetry, but it is clear that the urban world typically represented in Latin elegy bears some relation to Roman society in the late first century B.C.

If there was a new, younger and more liberal public for poetry in Tibullus' day, this was only one aspect of a gradual liberalization, or perhaps we should say a growing permissiveness, that had occurred in Roman society through the preceding century and a half. Roman writers never ceased harping on this theme, seeing the process as a sign and a cause of Rome's external difficulties. Social barriers of all kinds broke; a typical example is the slave who manages to make good and gain immense influence and wealth – Tibullus suggests (II.iii.63) that such is the origin of Nemesis' present keeper. One of the most obvious points was the change in the lives of Roman women. Roman women had at no time been as depressed a class as oriental or even Greek women, but within the Roman social structure their role was limited. Naturally it centred on marriage and the bearing of children, essential to the dynastic, economic and military future. Once married, the Roman girl changed her style of dress and put on with the *stola* of the *matrona* the inescapable concomitants of chastity, subordination, and dignified respectability. Not even her command of the household and her freedom to converse with men could keep this role acceptable to all women for ever. By the first century B.C., at least, Roman women had opened up the narrow confines of their lives considerably. Other standards of behaviour were much more commonly and openly on view in Rome. Roman women who had escaped from the ties of their class, and also foreigners, particularly Greek freedwomen, lived lives that were far from servile, sometimes in effect highly respectable and yet not obviously restricted. Roman poets could now write about women primarily as lovers, rather than breeders of their children, both because there were more women of whom this was true, and also because the actual marriage-customs had considerably relaxed their hold and so altered the general attitude. Divorce was now common, even among those to whom a dynastic marriage was still important; marriage on a *de facto* basis had increased in acceptability – cohabitation with intent to procreate became a legally valid tie after a certain lapse of time; freedmen and legionaries in the new regular army, now a significant percentage of the population, were not allowed a legal marriage and made the status of *contubernium* or concubinage an increasingly common phenomenon; equally important, women could now marry without submitting to the legal guardianship of their husbands. These changes were bound to alter the image of women as a class as well as their individual lives.

In Roman comedy of the third and early second centuries B.C. the women that young Romans fell in love with were slave-prostitutes – *meretrices*, who usually turned out, fortunately enough, to be free-born and therefore recoverable for society and marriage. In first-century poetry the women form a continuous spectrum from noble-born lady (e.g. Catullus' Clodia, and perhaps Sulpicia herself) through mistresses, courtesans, and prostitutes. But the typical courtesan of elegy is not usually a slave or a *meretrix* according the definition of the law, which required such women to register with the city magistrates, but either free-born or a freedwoman (the one exception to this is perhaps the 'whore' of III.xvi who apparently also works at spinning or weaving wool like Delia's slaves in I.iii). Whether free-born or freedwoman a Roman woman was legally required to be under the protection of a man. If this protector was not her father or husband, he would have to be a *tutor* or guardian. In the case of a courtesan this guardian might act as her keeper, pimp, common-law husband (complaisant or otherwise) or merely be a legal convenience and not come into the picture at all.

There was little moral stigma attaching to such a life; the class-stigma attached to being a freedwoman was a much greater reality, and for well-born men to associate with such women was only frowned on as a desertion of the dynastic aims of their class; Augustus' attempt to reinforce the Roman upper classes with laws designed to promote and protect marriage and pro-creation naturally emphasized this desertion. Where we find poets expressing a sense of moral disgrace, as in Propertius, and to a lesser extent Tibullus, it is because the nature of the love they portrayed came too near the degrading condition of slavery.

In the particular case of the Delia of Tibullus' first book, she is shown as having a *vir* (I.ii.43 and I.vi.8) – best translated as 'husband', though not necessarily implying any one particular legal status. Tibullus also pictures her as possibly having a chaperone (I.iii.83) – a figure like the nurse in Euripides' *Hippolytus* whose task is at different times both to protect and to procure. In I.iii the chaperone is pictured at the head of a full establishment of slave-girls who give the household an air of great respectability, like Penelope's in the Odyssey (I.iii.87). The 'divorce' of I.v.1 is only a divorce in practice – Delia is not represented as married to Tibullus in any legal sense; she has certainly not taken on the Roman married woman's dress (I.vi. 67–8); but then again, if she had lived with him as he had hoped she would continue to do, a kind of common-law marriage was implied by 'the treaty of our secret bed' (I.v.7.) Finally in I.vi.58 we are given a glimpse of Delia's old mother, here herself acting the role of procuress. What better way (in ancient Rome) for a poor widow to keep a respectable household solvent? – so Tibullus' tone invites us to feel. The picture may be sentimental, but the alternative prospect is frighteningly drawn a few lines later (I.vi.77). These details do not add up to a 'biography' of Delia, and need not even be self-consistent, but each one must have some sort of credibility in its context.

Tibullus' second book seems to show a debt to Propertius' first book, with its rather greater emphasis on the pain and degradation love can bring. Nemesis, like Propertius' Cynthia, can be very wild and cruel. However, whereas Cynthia seems to be well-born and cultured, Nemesis is represented as the most grasping of prostitutes, especially in II.iv. For this Tibullus puts the blame on her procuress, whose name Phryne suggests a Greek slave or freedwoman. Lygdamus' Neaera is, like Cynthia, a 'docta puella', pleased by nothing more than a book for a birthday present. It seems that the mark of an eligible female companion for many men was a degree of culture. Conversely it seems that the new public for poetry very much overlapped with the world of the figures represented in the poems, including young people like Pholoe and Marathus as well as *doctae puellae*. Lygdamus persistently speaks of Neaera as his wife, and their relationship as a marriage. This is not just metaphor. Here we have a picture of what was perhaps an increasingly common phenomenon – a marriage undertaken for love or emotional security. Because this is the only basis for the marriage, the contract is a very weak one, readily broken by either party. Neaera has not submitted to Lygdamus' legal guardianship, and no dowry affects the issue, though it is stressed that she comes from a normal, humane and friendly home (III.iv.92–4). Again in the case of Sulpicia and Cerinthus it is significant that though a marriage quite acceptable to Sulpicia's noble family is contemplated, the relationship depicted is wholly the relationship of lovers.

I have referred previously to the Tibullan ideal of love. It seems to me that in this field, if one may call it that, Tibullus made a very original and quite a surprising contribution. The idea of pure unfettered love was not new, and other poets had written idealistically of married love. Nor was it new to dwell on the pain of desertion by lover or mistress. Both Catullus' and Propertius' sensibilities were deeply affected by this guise of love. But to the sensibility of the Tibullan circle not just the promiscuity of one lover, but the very notion of promiscuity, in marriage or out of it, was repugnant (I.vi.67; III.ii.1; III.iv.80, 84ff.). The reason for this is partly the necessity to look beyond youth for security in the future (I.vi.77ff.). For this reason a relationship of trust (I.vi.75) and *true*, not only chaste or faithful, love (I.vi.86) is essential. We could be reading a description of the 'romantic' ideals of twentieth century Britain. Lygdamus also comes up with the idea that if his marriage with Neaera will not work they can continue to have a brother-sister relationship (III.i.23ff.). The ideal appears finally in fairly banal form in III.xix (of doubtful authorship). Propertius had written similarly of Cynthia. The lines strangely anticipate the clichés of many a song from the heyday of Romantic Love:

> You are my repose from care, you, even in blackest night,
>  Are light to me, you, in a desolation, are my company.
>
> (III.xix.11-12)

But at its highest the Tibullan ideal surely adds something new to the poetry of the age.


## (vi) 'Pastoral' and the Religious Background

The background to Tibullus' loves is half rural and half urban. This in itself reflects the division of time between town and country in the lives of most well-to-do Romans – time, that is, not devoted to service abroad. Roman senators and other rich men owed their substance to the land they owned, and those who were good managers visited their farms, living comfortably for a while in the increasingly rich villas that constituted the farmhouses. Messalla's coming and going is reflected in Sulpicia's elegies, and in Tibullus (II.iii) Nemesis has accepted the invitation of a landed lover to his country estate. Apart from the needs of the farm, country life offered the pleasures of relaxation and hunting. Here again Sulpicia and the 'Garland of Sulpicia' give a more realistic picture of things than Tibullus; few Romans even of Tibullus' less elevated standing would actually –

> . . . sow the soft-stemmed vines in their season
> And stout fruit-trees with a practised hand.

> (I.i.7–8)

A woman in Delia's or Nemesis' position would not commonly so much as set foot in the country, let alone take part in the work of the farm. The younger, smarter Romans no doubt left estate-management to their more responsible elders, enjoying the drinking parties and the group activities (see especially I.iv.11–12, 49–52) based on the city for as much of the year as possible. But all those not bound to the city for a living must have spent some time in the country and witnessed the rustic activities and the country festivals that Tibullus describes. Other times of the year might need to be spent at a health-resort such as Baiae or Tibur; these spas were centres of gay social life; the mournful Lygdamus actually contrasts their gaiety with his invalid gloom (III.v).

Tibullus' slightly unrealistic picture of country life is of course a very important part of what we mean when we call him a pastoral poet. His picture combines some of the realities with the security, companionship, and creativity which he perhaps found incompatible with the city. All his representations of country life are also imbued with a strong sense of the religious.

The very first poem in Book I is in the nature of a prayer and a promise – a prayer for the fulfilment of these pastoral longings of his, and a promise of attention to various divinities of the countryside if his request is fulfilled. The poem is in this way an epitome of Roman religion. A prayer coupled with a promise, both ideas being contained in the Latin word *votum*, and then the fulfilment of that promise, usually a sacrifice or dedicatory offering, constitute the one single and constant activity on which Roman religion was founded for the ordinary people. There was no religion in the most common modern sense – a cult with an orthodox creed or a theologically derived ethic. Roman priests were there to conduct this basic activity on behalf of the state or other public bodies. Their sacrifices perhaps took a more ritualized form than those of individuals, and were often performed in conjunction with the art of divination, but otherwise they had no public mission either of pastoral care or to proselytize.

The divinities addressed in Tibullus' prayer accurately reflect the fluid theology of this religion. First of all there are the purely Italian gods, whose worship dates back to the early agricultural days of Rome's history, and is peculiar to the native Roman religion. First among these are the *Lares*, the 'protectors of (the) ... estate'. The Lares were particularly associated with the crossings of the paths that separated one estate from another, but were also worshipped inside the house, which frequently contained a Lararium, a little shrine or altar for offerings to be made or incense burned by members of the household. The cross-roads stones mentioned in I.i.12 may have something to do with the Lares, although cross-roads were also associated with the Underworld and its gods. Similarly the veneration of isolated tree-stumps is a practice that dates right back to the days when the primitive agriculturalists saw spirits everywhere, concerned with all their activities, incomprehensibly opposing them or helping, and needing constant appeasement. Some of the other gods of Tibullus' prayer probably had their origins in this period, but by classical times had had grafted to them features of Greek religion. Ceres for example is originally a spirit of the cereal crop; but Tibullus could not have avoided being aware of the Greek goddess Demeter with whom Ceres had been identified, and in fact he describes Ceres in typically Greek anthropomorphic and pictorial terms as a straw-haired lady. We also hear of 'peaceful Pales'. Originally the word Pales was probably a plural referring to the spirits of the flocks and herds, but again Pales has become personalized and made singular (though never firmly fixing on one sex or the other) under the influence of the Greeks, who preferred single patron deities. The god Priapus is a foreign importation. He was originally worshipped locally at Lampsacus in Asia Minor, but his cult, through the universal significance of his chief appendage, the phallus, spread to Greece and thence to Rome. He appears in I.iv in one of his traditional roles, that of the adviser on sexual technique, and here in another, as a scarecrow in a garden, protecting the fertility of the earth, but scaring the birds 'with his cruel sickle'.

Lastly, Tibullus is happy to make his appeal to much vaguer divinities of his own creation. He addresses his 'hopes' in I.i; in another poem (I.x) he makes much of 'Peace'. In this way he was actually able to make a personal addition to Roman religion, not like a theologian, of course, in order to promote the Truth for others, but to satisfy his own religious instincts. And it is his personal religious instinct that does infuse these poems with a particular quality not found elsewhere in classical literature. II.ii is a good example of what I mean. The name Natalis rightly refers to the spirit that attends each man's birth. It is thus hardly dissociable from a man's *Genius*, or guardian-spirit (the name is etymologically connected with 'generation'). The reverence Tibullus expresses for these divinities gives us a deep sense of the individual human destiny of Cornutus, and the sanctity of this occasion in his life. Next after these two Tibullus introduces the deity Love. In Latin the god of Love or at least of falling-in-love was Amor or Cupido, in Greek Eros – all three personified abstracts (Venus, more often mentioned by Tibullus, like Aphrodite, more nearly corresponds to the abstract idea of Sex). In Hellenistic art Eros had collected wings and a bow and arrows, symbols much played on by other Latin poets. But although Tibullus' Amor here flies on 'fluttering pinions', the character he is given is peculiar to Tibullus and somehow quite different from the more conventional Cupid of II.i.66ff. or the opening of II.vi. This 'Love' is an abstract that owes most to what Tibullus personally felt about marriage and conjugal love – the context makes this plain. The whole poem is deeply religious in feeling, but religious in the Roman sense. It breathes awareness of the presence of extra-human forces or spirits, but somehow the reaction is not one of dread, but of reverence mixed with an affection throroughly appropriate on an occasion when all has been or is being done to honour the spirits concerned, and their presence can therefore be nothing but a blessing to the unanimously favourable gathering.

A similar, though less intense, religious feeling pervades II.i and a section of II.v, both of which actually describe communal country festivals. II.v.87ff. seems to be a fairly straight description of the festival known as the Parilia, held in honour of Pales. The purpose of the ceremony was to purify sheep and sheepfolds and to ward off disease in the future. Tibullus' description shows the festival to be primitive enough in its ritual details. What interests Tibullus more is the family atmosphere – children allowed to be affectionately cheeky with their parents, and the grandfather indulging his grandson. True to his calling as an elegiac poet, Tibullus responds to the poignancy of the moment, the sweet pain of the young people going too far and then making up their quarrel. But we never forget that this is only happening because it is a special occasion; the details of the ritual fire-leaping and the turf tables and couches are there to remind us. What actual ceremony is depicted in II.i. is not so clear. Possibly only a general effect is intended, with details from more than one festival. The poem begins in a solemn, almost ritual mode, which immediately establishes the communal religious context. However, the poem gains depth from the vignettes of country life and love which are inserted into the framework of the festi-val. These digressions fall into a more traditional and perhaps deliberately artificial vein; the effect is to add fresh dimensions to the original picture; the transitions are so smoothly worked that Tibullus makes us feel a real continuity between the pro-fane love of the elegists and the religion of the country people.

The first of these two poems, II.v, is much concerned with the practice I have briefly referred to above – divination. The Greeks and other peoples had perceived omens in dreams and all sorts of other natural phenomena, including unusual incidents that occurred in the course of sacrifices; the performances of birds in particular were studied. All these took their place in Roman religion, and are referred to as the province of Apollo and his priests (see II.v.11–14; also I.viii.3ff., III.iv.45–8). II.v.14 specifically describes the practice of haruspication, or divining the future from the state of the entrails of sacrificed animals. This was a particularly Italian art and seems to have been developed to a high degree of sophistication by the Etrus-cans. Not only did private individuals try to get knowledge of the future through divination (see e.g. I.iii.11–20), but it also played an important part in public religion. No serious enter-prise could be entered on, at least in earlier times, without waiting until favourable omens were perceived. As a further help there were sacred writings which could be consulted. These sacred writings, known as the Sibylline books, were thought to have been presented to Rome by the Sibyl of Cumae in the time of the kings. A Sibyl simply means a wise woman; II.v.65ff. lists some other famous Sibyls. However the original Sibylline books had come into Rome's possession, they had certainly been added to over the centuries with other Sibylline writings culled from the various religious centres throughout the Mediterranean area traditionally connected with Sibyls. This poem, II.v, in fact celebrates the election of Messalla's son Messalinus to the board of *quindecimviri sacris faciundis*, one of whose chief tasks was the revision and recension of this body of prophetic material. Tibullus uses the opportunity to take a backward glance at the importance of prophecy in the early legends of Rome, in particular the legend of Aeneas (perhaps already becoming more familiar to Romans, as Virgil's nascent *Aeneid* became known). In so doing, he was, of course, acting very much in accordance with the wish of Augustus to revive Roman religion, and through the arts to give new life to her ritual and moral traditions. This poem in fact gets nearer than any other of his works to being national poetry. But of course the poem goes on from these themes of national prophecies and portents to the description of the country festival I have already discussed; and from there to purely private themes (l.109 ff.). The poem actually culminates, just before the final appeal to Apollo, in a picture of Messalla making an 'exhibition of fatherly love'. It is almost as if Tibullus, as an elegiac poet, feels compelled to return via his own personal experience, to the personal and private significance of the event which his poem celebrates. The final appeal to Augustus' patron god, Apollo, is not to Apollo the augur or Augustus' patron deity, the saviour of the state at the battle of Actium, but to the beautiful and gracious brother of the chaste Diana.

Tibullus does not only describe his native and national religion, but gives us also fascinating glimpses of other areas of religion. Nearest to home, perhaps, was the practice of magic. A belief in spells, curses, and potions forms a part of most primitive religions. Many of the magic practices and superstitions that survived in Tibullus' day no doubt had native roots. A good example of the kind of primitive practice that has passed into the instinctive behaviour of the people is the practice of spitting to ward off the bad influence or infection of another man's misfortune (I.ii.97–8). But in most of Tibullus' references to magic it is simply a question of a witch being called in for help in a love-affair (I.ii.44ff., I.v.12ff., and I.viii.17ff.). These witches are literary hybrids, with an unmistakable Greek ancestry. The archetypal Greek witch is Medea, who dropped her box of herbs in her flight through Thessaly, it was said; and sure enough these witches work with Thessalian herbs and poisons, or else spells, such as those actually represented in a famous poem by the Greek Theocritus, later imitated by Virgil.[11] An eastern element is suggested by the clashing gongs or cymbals (I.viii.18–21ff.) used to prevent the moon being pulled down – traditionally the ultimate demonstration of the power of magic. In fact, by Tibullus' time, the actual practice of magic was an international phenomenon, used for a multiplicity of ends, including, no doubt, tricks like transplanting a neighbour's crops into your own field (I.viii.19), which must be as old as agriculture itself. It ties up with Greco-Roman religion to the extent that it was connected with the worship of underworld deities, particularly Hecate and Diana, both also connected, significantly enough, with the moon. Many people no doubt believed implicitly in magic, particularly as it affected personal relationships, but Tibullus' treatment of it is literary and artificial compared with his treatment of the rural Italian religion; it becomes a stage-prop in the setting for love-affairs.

Somewhere between magic and the country religion on the scale of Tibullus' involvement come the Egyptian and oriental

11. Theocritus: *Idylls*, II; Virgil: *Eclogues*, VIII.

mystery-religions. Foreign slaves and foreign influence had flowed steadily into the ever more urbanized city of Rome ever since the time of the Punic wars in the third century B.C. Cults and religions accompanied them; first the Greek, for example the orgiastic worship of Bacchus/Dionysus and the Greek mystery-cults; also the worship of the Great Mother goddess of Asia Minor who reappears in various guises and under various names from ever further eastwards (e.g., Ops of Ida – I.iv.68); eventually the cults of Isis and Serapis, and others not mentioned by Tibullus, such as Mithras. It was inevitable that as city-life grew more sophisticated and separate from the country, the simple country-based religion would seem increasingly inadequate. Some were content to add to it, to graft on to it features of other religions that seemed more appropriate, or add new abstract deities to its worship, as we have seen Tibullus himself doing. An example of such adaptation was the cult of Fortuna; the name had originally had an agricultural significance, but was adopted by the uprooted city-dwellers to signify abstract Chance, and was by this time endowed with splendid temples in several Italian cities (see III.iii.22). Another city-dwellers' religion was the cult of Isis, whose temples appeared in cities as far afield as London. In Tibullus this is the religion followed by Delia. We learn some details in I.iii.23ff.; the mention of the painted tablets hung up in the temple, recording prayers granted and successful cures, gives us a hint of the popularity of this religion. Typically enough an initiation into the mysteries of Isis does not discourage Delia from asking at all the other shrines for oracles and omens (I.iii.9–10). The connection of many foreign religions with various forms of divination seems to have been strong. We get a fearsome picture of the frenzied priestess of the Cappadocian goddess Bellona in I.vi.45ff., whom Tibullus has consulted about the future.

Tibullus is impressed by these religions. They naturally

occur to him when he thinks of impieties or ritual impurities he may be suffering for. But he always seems to want to move away from them in the poems back to the religion of his home and country. His appeal to Isis (I.iii.27ff.) is followed by a prayer to be reunited with his Lares; this is followed again by an idealistic description of the golden days of pre-agricultural Italy – when Saturnus ruled. This kind of movement underlies the pattern of the whole of I.vii. A large section of this poem is concerned with the myth of the Egyptian Osiris (ll.23–48). Osiris is identified both with the Nile itself, and the sacred white ox kept at Memphis, which in life represented the bull-god Apis, but when dead and replaced by another bull was mourned for as Osiris. With the many inventions attributed to him, which particularly suggest a parallel with the Roman Bacchus, the figure of Osiris becomes a poetic symbol of great complexity. He is introduced into the poem in the context of Messalla's foreign conquests. Finally he is invited to come and join the celebrations held on Messalla's birthday in honour of his Genius, or guardian-spirit. The rest of the poem is purely Italian in setting; Messalla has returned from abroad and will now settle as an honoured *paterfamilias* where his roots are – but with a halo of glory from his exploits abroad. Like everything else in Tibullus, the treatment of religion suggests a strong movement away from the brutal exterior and urban world, back to the ideal Italian countryside. Sometimes this seems mere quietism, but at his best, as in this poem, I think, Tibullus achieves a more comprehensive view.

## (vii) Tibullus' Style and Qualities

Enough has now perhaps been said about the historical background to the poems. In writing about this I have in fact said much of what I want to say about the meaning of the poetry. I hope to have shown that his treatment of themes of love, and particularly of religious feeling is individual and original, and that he would be worth our attention if for nothing else for the insight he gives us into the tensions between town and country, the present and the past, and war and peace, that existed in Augustan Rome. But there are a few things that must be said about the quality of Tibullus' poetry and that of the other poets in the collection, and arising out of that about the aims of this translation.

The virtues of the Tibullan style are perhaps not virtues very highly rated today. We very understandably find the abrupt transitions, the bejewelled surface and the sheer intensity of Propertius more expressive and stimulating. Ovid is clearly more *entertaining*. Quintilian[12] described Tibullus' style once and for all in the words *tersus atque elegans* – 'clean and elegant'. The achievement of elegance in Latin is in effect the liberating of its virtues of simplicity, conciseness, clarity, niceness of emphasis, directness of expression – one could probably continue the list – by the elimination of its corresponding vices. At least that is the picture one gets from a look at the development of the literature (and I suppose also from an education in Latin composition). Such elegance will exemplify the quality classical scholars have always referred to as Latinity. Clearly the English language now has less affinity with pure *Latinitas* than it did even two or three hundred years ago.

How does this work out in practice? The techniques of Latin poetry are very much concerned with selecting and arranging words expressively within each individual line. It is a large part of Tibullus' elegance that we rarely feel that he is doing this mechanically or failing to respond to his vocabulary; clarity is

12. Quintilian: *Institutio Oratoria*, X.i.93.

never sacrificed. Consider for a moment the opening lines of II.i:

> Quisquis adest, faveat: fruges lustramus et agros,
>   ritus ut a prisco traditus extat avo.
> Bacche, veni, dulcisque tuis e cornibus uva
>   pendeat, et spicis tempora cinge, Ceres.
> luce sacra requiescat humus, requiescat arator,
>   et grave suspenso vomere cesset opus.
> solvite vincla iugis: nunc ad praesepia debent
>   plena coronato stare boves capite.

How clear and simple the words look on the page – the objects and actions of farm life so clearly presented. Yet it is not flat and predictable, as these words suggest. The basic vocabulary of Latin poetry has a lot of in-built metonomy, where a word that originally stands for a feature of some concept, or a related idea, is made to do duty for the original concept. In line 5, for example, the Latin has *luce sacra; luce* basically means *light*, hence *dawn* or *daylight* or the *day* we see dawning. Thus the combination of *luce* with *sacra* (dedicated or holy) produces a direct pictorial effect which our perhaps over-sophisticated English vocabulary cannot easily represent. A greater human involvement is often suggested, because of the tendency of Latin verbs to imply personal subjects; in line 6 *cesset* conveys the idea of *people* lying idle, as well as telling us that the work is to cease. Tibullus always seems to use the simple nuances of such words appropriately and to maximum effect.

Nor is he merely master of the technique of writing clear and simple Latin. We find in him examples of the more clever types of word-play and onomatopoeia that had become almost second nature to the poets of the Augustan period. Take for example:

> namque agor ut per plana citus sola verbere turben
>
> (I.v.3)

The rhythm and the predominant consonants brilliantly suggest
the quick skittering of the top over a flat surface. See also –

> naufraga quam vasti tunderet unda maris
>
> (II.iv.10)

– for the noise of breakers; and not only the sound, but also the
devious and, for once, artificially extended word-chain of –

> an te, Cydne, canam, tacitis qui leniter undis
> caeruleus placidis per vada serpis aquis, . . .
>
> (I.vii.13–14)

– which echoes the long windings of the stream through its
lagoon. But examples like this do not often stand out on Tibullus'
pages. The felicities one notices are more often small matters
of the precise placing of a word, or an unsuspected image con-
jured up by an innocent juxtaposition. I use the word 'image'
guardedly; it must be stressed that Tibullus, even compared
with other Latin poets, uses very little simile and metaphor,
factors so crucial when critics discuss the imagery of Shakespeare
or even Virgil. (This may be what Quintilian means when he
describes him as *tersus* – 'clean'.) What we so often get from
Tibullus is a sudden visual flash when he has described something
just that little bit more pictorially or suggestively than he would
ever need to if he were writing in prose. To add more examples
to those I have quoted:

> . . . quos . . .
> Solis et admotis inficit ignis equis:
>
> (II.iii.59–60)

(The horses of the Sun-god swoop low to dye the easterners'
skins.)

> . . . et fleat effusis ante sepulcra comis
>
> (I.iii.8)

46

Not only is the girl's hair *effusus* – allowed to flow unrestrainedly – but so are her tears, and her very manner of weeping; the way the words are arranged cannot help suggesting this.

These are some of the ways in which Tibullus displays his elegance. But Ovid is also elegant, one might point out, and so are some English poets, such as Pope, a very classical writer. And yet Tibullus' style is very different overall from theirs. In the first place, the quality of wit is much less pronounced in Tibullus than in Ovid or Pope. Tibullus hardly ever plays with the language; the nearest he gets is the kind of rather bitter pun we find in I.x.2:

> quam ferus et vere ferreus ille fuit!

(What a brute he was, truly a brute-steel-hearted man!)

Examples of his wit are nearly all in the same general line – showing up the ridiculousness of love and those in love. II.vi keeps breaking into this vein (though it gets more serious as it proceeds); lines 11–12 are typical:

> I speak grand words – but when I've grandly done so,
> A closed door immediately dashes my brave remarks.

Other examples are the picture of Apollo in love in II.iii (cf. III.iv.68), and the pathetic description of the teacher of love who finds his own teaching useless to himself – I.iv.83–4 (cf.I.ii.89f.). This positively ironic vein merges into the generally wry tone in which he often describes his predicament, e.g. I.v.1–2. This kind of wit is very far from the persistent play on words and metre which characterizes Ovid.

Tibullus is different from Ovid in another very important respect – the pattern of his thought. Ovid's elegies typically take a single starting-point, and then range fairly systematically over the different ideas it suggests; he presents a clear 'argument'. Tibullus does not subject us to consistent argument at all; he moves quietly and unobtrusively on to discuss different matters with an effect that can at times seem like aimlessness. Each idea seems only to be suggested by the one before it, and sometimes even then only by an inessential aspect of that idea. I.iii may serve as an example of the Tibullan method. Diving into the poem at intervals one finds him writing successively about his own funeral, looking for omens before his departure for Corfu, Delia as a devotee of Isis, the 'Saturnian age' in Italy, the Elysian fields, the punishment of sinners in the Underworld, and finally his projected reunion with Delia. But Tibullus is not merely presenting a series of pictures. Connections are made or at least suggested. Sometimes the connections are obvious, as, for example, the contrast between his descriptions of the Elysian fields and 'the home of evil'. Other connections are made by a series of quick steps – talking about the age of Saturn brings to mind by contrast the current age, that of Jupiter, the mark of which is violence and premature death even for the innocent, who will, of course, go to the Elysian fields: it is all rather breathtaking. Sometimes the link between two sections is logical enough, but Tibullus insists on arriving by apparently roundabout or inconsequential means. Thus his sickness and funeral described in the opening lines may well be the direct consequence, the poem suggests, of the displeasure of Cupid, a possibility which he and Delia did not take into account when they were looking for omens before his departure – but consider the pivot on which the poem turns to this second point:

> . . . no mother here . . . no sister here . . .
>> Delia's not here, who asked each shrine, they say,
>> For oracles, before I went away.

The connection is made purely through the mention of Delia in the first context, which is made to lead in to her part in the second.

48

One sometimes feels with Tibullus (particularly if one has just been reading Ovid, or any poet with a more linear cast of mind) that he is ranging over these diverse and often very conventional themes in a rather aimless way. This is particularly so in the poems which include dramatic elements. Here again our other reading is liable to condition our expectations. I.ii, for example, begins with a dramatized appeal to someone to 'strengthen the wine'. If we have been reading Propertius or Ovid or even the Odes of Horace we may well expect Tibullus to maintain the dramatic situation he has conjured up in this opening. An excellent example of a dramatic situation being maintained can be seen in Lygdamus' III.vi which begins by presenting the poet in a very similar situation. Lygdamus' poem preserves this dramatic setting throughout – the boy is again being asked to pour wine in the last few lines, and the poem is mostly about the power of Bacchus. Tibullus by contrast has left the subject of wine by line 5 and never returns to it. To him the dramatized mood of escapism is only one of the many themes he wants to present. Similarly the religious atmosphere of II.i is largely created by the dramatic presentation of a ritual command in the first two lines:

All present, keep holy silence; we cleanse the fields and the harvest,
　To re-enact the ceremony our fathers handed down.

But we go wrong if we expect the whole poem to fit the lips of an officiating priest.

Once we realize that Tibullus' thought-patterns are consistently of this type it becomes clear what their intended effect is. Tibullus is deliberately echoing the transitions of actual thinking (i.e. not the convention of dramatic monologue). Elegiac poetry is not simply a matter of writing autobiographically, but of giving a convincing and artistically satisfying picture of personal responses. So Tibullus tries to represent real thinking in a convincing manner, but at the same time submits his subject matter to fairly rigid control. His poems are not mere random fantasias on a rag-bag of themes. I have already suggested some of the ways in which he uses his transitions and his range of themes to create whole poems. Ultimately one can only summarize this very vaguely by saying, for example: I.iii presents a unified expression of the poet's response to the implications of sickness, and the tension between the security of faithful love and the risks of worldly involvement, or: II.v glorifies a personal commitment to the religious traditions of Rome, but ultimately suggests a movement back from the urban scene to the roots of family life and the countryside. The very elegance of the original creation discourages one from saying even this much, and the summaries tend to stress unduly the similarities of plot in these poems. It is necessary to challenge the idea that they have no unity, are not about anything; but the delight of Tibullus' poetry lies in the mode, the constantly shifting pattern that life presents in his thoughts.

This is achieved not merely by the subtle transition from one subject to another, but also by the constant variation of grammatical subject and syntax. Consider the number of grammatical subjects and the transitions from one to the other in the first fourteen lines of I.x.:

> *Who* first introduced . . . ?
>> What a brute *he* was . . . !
> . . . *murder* . . . *war* . . .
>> The shorter *way* . . .
> Or is *the man* innocent . . . *we* being the ones
>> . . .
>
> *This* is surely the fault . . . there were no *wars*
>> When the cup . . .
> There were no *strongholds* . . . *Pales* . . . the *shepherd* . . .
>> . . .

50

If *I* . . . *I* . . .
. . .

But as it is *I* . . . and some enemy *soldier* . . . etc.

Latin handles some of the changes of subject much more easily than English can; we are back with Latinity here again. Consider:

an nihil *ille* miser meruit, *nos* ad mala nostra . . .

(I.x.5)

(Or is the man innocent, to be pitied rather, we being the ones . . .)

The antithesis of the two phrases is enough to supply the train of thought; in English we need a 'whereas', or its equivalent. The opening of I.i is an even more complex example of this kind of variation, though here it has to do with Tibullus' use of the moods and tenses of the Latin verb – less accessible to the English reader. However something of the complexity of the original can be judged by considering the variations in the English verbs needed to try and capture all the shades of the Latin: 'The amassing . . . I leave to others . . . let them be terrified . . . their sleep routed . . . I would have poverty lead me . . . so long as my hearth glows . . . I'll be . . . never desert me . . . because I am . . . the first-fruits are laid up . . . a wreath must hang . . . etc.' All this is not perversity on Tibullus' part, nor does the variety of his subjunctive usages reveal a desire to give future linguistic pedants something to chew on. They are used to conjure up possibilities in the mind, reflecting the way we play with ideas, not facts; or rather ideas related to a rather random collection of facts. As we read we share with the poet a sense of the infinite shades of experience.

## (*viii*) *The Tibullan Poets*

Lygdamus' style cannot maintain the level of Tibullus' elegance. Where the arrangement of the words in a Tibullan pentameter always seems simple, natural and yet expressive, Lygdamus often seems over-complex. See, for example:

> blandaque cum multa tura dedisse prece
>
> (III.iii.2)

Here he has arranged the words in text-book pattern, but the epithets 'blanda' and 'multa' are too vague to give the kind of clear, checkered cross-pattern Tibullus usually achieves. Lygdamus will allow noun and epithet on the other hand to fall too flatly together:

> aurataeque trabes marmoreumque solum
>
> (III.iii.16)

Sometimes he merely pads his lines with unnecessary words, e.g. *ante* in III.i.10. Occasionally he plays with word repetitions to good pathetic effect:

> Qui primus caram iuveni carumque puellae
>   eripuit iuvenem . . .
>
> (III.ii.1–2)

– but sometimes to no effect at all. These technical details are important, because ultimately the style of Lygdamus' poems is not very different from the Tibullan style. It is true, as I have pointed out, that III.vi, for example, maintains a consistent dramatic setting, and that each poem constitutes a much more obvious unity than Tibullus' do. But then four of the six are really very short; and the other two are curiously static – the thought and the dramatic situation never develop. Lygdamus therefore depends for his effect largely on the details of his language. Writing slightly later than Tibullus, as we may judge from his birth-date, he has kept up with some of the poetic developments of the time, and in particular learnt from Propertius. The mythological insets (e.g. III.iii.23–24, 39–40) and the use of striking and picturesque vocabulary bear witness to this. At best Lygdamus can create a strong visual impression and an effective atmosphere, as in much of III.iv. His best poem is surely III.v where he successfully blends these elements with the Tibullan manner; the thought pattern moves a little more freely, and instead of dwelling solely on his own plight, he brings life to the poem by the consistent contrast between his situation at death's door and the life at Tibur. (Is the poem really addressed to Neaera? Perhaps the anonymity of the addressee is part of the intended effect.)

The panegyric of Messalla, III.vii, is indeed a very poor poem. It is in the hexameter metre throughout, but with its frequent and uncontrolled enjambments might as well be in any other metre for all the difference it makes. Lines 39–44 and 82–105 are examples of the writer's prosaic and graceless style. Some passages rise I suppose to a higher level. I particularly like the description of the moment when the sacrificer receives his omens (III.vii.118–134). There is a freshness in the way the scene is put together, despite the derivative style of the individual lines.

The 'Garland of Sulpicia' (III.viii–xii) comes nearer to the unaffected elegance of Tibullus' attested work than do the poems of Lygdamus. Sometimes there is a slight monotony, as in the pentameters of III.x, far too many of which are based on exactly the same word-pattern: ... *Phoebe superbe* (l.2) ... *candida membra* (l.6) ... *corpora fessa* (l.10) ... *aspera verba* (l.14) ... *salva puella* (l.16) ... *credula turba* (l.18). However, this effect may just possibly be intended, to support the comforting, lulling tone of the poem. Here again the author has preferred to write short poems of some unity than to follow the Tibullan method. But they do seem to have been written consciously as a group. Not only do they take their subject-matter from Sulpicia's group of short poems, but they are actually arranged so that the two poems written in the person of Sulpicia (III.ix and xi) are framed by three written in the person of the sympathetic by-stander. The drama that the poet has created by this means has a lot of life in it.

The last two poems in the collection need no further comment, and I can therefore end with Sulpicia. Immediately one can observe in her tiny poems a distinct style. The main distinction is the convolution of the sense. The very first couplet contains what is really a most complicated idea. The Latin, literally translated, says something like this: *at last has come a love such that the reputation of covering it up would be more of a shame to me than that of laying it bare to anyone*. This kind of complexity goes hand in hand with some very simple, almost naïve ideas, such as that in line four of the same poem:

> *Venus has brought him and put him in my lap.*

The diction is simple, almost colloquial at times. To me the effect of this style is most convincing. It seems immediately to suggest the naïve young girl suddenly growing up to complexity of thought as she grapples with the ideas love has forced on her. It is true that there are linguistic and metrical awkwardnesses, and no one is going to claim that Sulpicia gave herself scope for greatness, but to dismiss these poems as suffering from the (inevitable) deficiencies of a female writer, seems to me at the very least to be wantonly missing a good thing.

How then is the translator to deal with the elegance and subtle transitions of Tibullus, and how is he to try and distinguish the contributions of the other poets in this collection? I have given some examples of the way one has to try to cope with the shifts of mood and subject in Tibullus – inevitably with much less elegance than one would like. Fortunately the actual content – the pictures and ideas contained in the individual sentences – is so clear that it will probably come across. The crucial question is that of style and form. I hope to have shown that the elegiac couplet is, in no condemnatory sense, an artificial verse-style. In general the effect of the metre is one of conciseness and a kind of dry wit. It has been strongly argued that the only logical way to reproduce this in English is with a concise metre, also conducive to the expression of wit, such as the rhymed or heroic couplet. There is a lot in this argument. But the heroic couplet is indelibly stamped in English with the mark of Alexander Pope. Essays in this form tend to sound as if they are trying to emulate Pope whatever steps one takes to try and prevent this. It is particularly true when one faces the fact that it is almost impossible to pack another poet's sense into this form without occasionally resorting to techniques of inversion in order to secure a rhyme. Finally, of course, the ten-syllabled lines of the heroic couplet are just too short for the English to do justice to more than a percentage of the Latin. Nevertheless, so strong in my mind is the need to remember the comparative artificiality and conventionality of Latin elegiac verse that I have tried to have it both ways. Five of Tibullus' elegies have been put into rhymed couplets to act as a corrective on the reading of the rest, which are rendered in less stringent forms. Naturally I have tried to avoid inversions or irretrievably archaic vocabulary, and I have also selected for this treatment the five elegies (I.ii, I.iii, I.viii, I.ix and II.iii) which I think lose least and gain most by it. In some the speed of the English couplet gives the necessary bounce to comparatively conventional subject-matter, and in others it underlines their consistently lighter tone. The remaining poems are likewise not translated to any uniform scheme, but treated as I thought they individually demanded.

When I came to the other poets, the difficulty was to differentiate not only their styles, but also the quality of their language, without positively attempting to write bad English. In Lygdamus' case I have tried deliberately a more pretentious manner and a less traditional approach to the flow of the rhythm. The Panegyric (III.vii) seemed to call for a kind of garrulous and shapeless blank verse – here I feel the difference in quality should be clear. Sulpicia's convolutions suggested some sort of unobtrusive rhyme scheme or half-rhyme scheme and I thought the poems were short enough to allow me to rhyme across the couplets for a change. For the 'Garland of Sulpicia' I could think of no positively appropriate distinguishing technique – I just hope I have felt my way to something that will echo the blandness and slight grace of the originals. The aim is of course to make all these poems interesting without ever overshadowing the much more considerable achievements of Tibullus.

## (ix) Some Books on Tibullus

It is perhaps not surprising that Tibullus has always been more popular on the continent than in this country, and particularly so in France. French elegance is clearly closer to Tibullan Latinity than English word-magic. A glance at any scholarly bibliography will show how disproportionately greater an amount of print has been devoted to Tibullus abroad than at home. Even so Tibullus and the other poets of the collection have had an almost negligible amount of direct influence on subsequent literature. Donne in his Elegies and Goethe in his Roman Elegies turned mainly to Ovid for their models. André Chénier is one of the only poets of note whose works bear traces of Tibullan inspiration – lines from Lygdamus are imitated, interestingly enough, almost as often as Tibullus. The fact is that, although

Tibullus may have been the first to introduce many of the tradi-
tional themes of Roman elegy, his successors in the field nearly
always took up these themes and put them to much greater
dramatic effect, or expressed them either more forcibly or more
wittily. Tibullus' influence will always be an indirect one – as a
model of sophisticated simplicity and craftsmanship. If his
lines are not quoted by great men, it is probably because he is
not the kind of poet from whom we get revelations of truth. But
the early reading of Tibullus along with Julius Caesar perhaps
helps to give that intangible quality to education which teachers
of Classics are so anxious to preserve today.

Not much is available to the English reader on the subject of
Tibullus and his circle. The edition of K. F. Smith (reprinted
1962) has a full introduction which discusses most of the prob-
lems (and includes a complete text of all the ancient sources on
Tibullus). Postgate, whose text these translations are based on,[13]
knew his Tibullus well enough, but his discussions are weighed
down with some rather dry controversy, much of it started by
himself. There is a comprehensive study of the genre – Georg
Luck's *The Latin Love Elegy* (2nd edn, 1969) – which has very
valuable chapters on Tibullus and the other poets of the group.
K. Quinn's *The Catullan Revolution* and his discussion of Pro-
pertius in *Latin Explorations* are also very valuable on the history
and aims of the genre. There is also an essay on Tibullus, 'Tersus
atque elegans', by J. P. Elder in *Critical Essays on Latin Litera-
ture, Elegy and Lyric* (edited by J. P. Sullivan). To all of these
works I am indebted for much of what I have written above. But
the best discussion of Tibullus' style and achievement seems

13. Where there are obvious lacunae or corrupt passages in the text I have
filled in the sense on the lines of the conjectures in Postgate's own (prose)
translation in the Loeb Classical Library edition. (I.ii.25, I.vi.76, II.iii.14a
and 75 – lacunae; I.ix.25 and III.vi.55 – corrupt text.) Lacunae are also
suggested at I.x.25, II.iii.34 and III.ix.4, but these seemed possible to ignore.

to me to be that in *Tradition and Originality in Roman Poetry* by Gordon Williams (1968); I did not read this until I had been living with Tibullus for some time; when I did, I found there, stated with the cool authority of real scholarship, nearly all the conclusions about Tibullus' art at which I had been tentatively arriving.

Most of the scholars and critics who have voiced an opinion give Tibullus a comparatively humble place in the history of Latin literature. Perhaps rightly. But living with this poetry has certainly taught me its qualities, and given me a pleasure I hardly expected at the outset.

Heaton Mersey 1971                    PHILIP DUNLOP

# BOOK ONE
# TIBULLUS

## I.i

The amassing of wealth in yellow gold I leave to others,
    And owning many acres of ploughed earth;
Let them be terrified by the enemy at the door and by persistent
        hardship,
    Their sleep routed by the blasts of the trumpet of war.
I would have poverty lead me along through a life of com-
    fort,
    So long as my hearth glows and my fire still burns.
I'll be a real farmer and sow the soft-stemmed vines in their
        season,
    And stout fruit-trees with a practised hand.
Never, my hopes, desert me, but always offer heaped-up harvests,
    And supply the rich must in brimming vats –
Because I am respectful of every lone tree-trunk in the plough-
    land
    That holds a wreath of flowers, and every old cross-roads
        stone;
And whatever the harvest that each new season produces,
    The first-fruits are laid up for the farmer-god;
Golden Ceres, for you from my farm a wreath of corn-ears
    Must hang on the outside of your temple doors;
And in the apple orchard be placed a red-painted guardian,
    A Priapus, with his cruel sickle to terrify the birds.
You too, once protectors of a prosperous estate, now of a poor
        one,
    You, my Lares, you also take your dues;
In those days a slaughtered heifer purified unnumbered bullocks:
    Now a lamb is the small victim for my tiny plot.

A lamb shall fall indeed for you, and round it the youth of the
     country
  Shall shout 'Hooray! – Give good harvest, and give good wine!'
As for me, just give me the chance to live content with a little,
  And not be always given over to long roads,
But to avoid the dog-star's summer risings in the shadow
  Under a tree by the banks of a passing stream;
Not ashamed at times, in fact, to manipulate a pitchfork,
  Or castigate the slow-moving oxen with a goad;
Not too fastidious to carry a lamb or a goat's suckling
  That its mother has forgotten, back to the house in my arms.
And you, spare my tiny flock, you wolves and robbers;
  A great big herd is where plunder should be sought;
For here each year I regularly purify my shepherd
  And sprinkle peaceful Pales with drops of milk.
Be near me, gods, and just because they come from a poor man's
     table
  And from clean earthen vessels, don't despise my gifts –
It was a farmer in days of old who first made goblets
  Of earthenware, and fashioned them out of the responsive
     clay.
I do not miss my ancestors' former wealth and the profit
  My forefathers got from the stored-up grain.
A small crop is enough; enough indeed to rest on a mattress,
  If I can, and refresh my limbs on my familiar bed.
How pleasant to hear the unbending gales from the bedroom,
  Holding my mistress in my unwarlike arms;
Or when a wintry Auster has poured out its icy waters,
  To pursue, with the rain's assistance, a carefree sleep.
This is all the luck I want; he may be the rich one rightly,
  Who can endure the madness of the sea and the unsmiling
     rains.
All the gold there is, and all the emeralds may perish,

Sooner than that any girl should weep for my journeyings.
It's right that you should go to war on land and sea, Messalla,
　So that your house can display the enemy spoils:
But the chains of a beautiful girl hold me fettered;
　In fact I sit as a porter at her stubborn door.
A good reputation, Delia, is none of my concern – provided
　I'm with you, I'm happy to be known as feckless and slow.
Let my eyes see you when my last hour approaches,
　Let me hold you with my weakening arms as I die.
You'll weep as I'm laid on the litter that's soon to be kindled,
　And cover me with kisses mixed with mourning tears.
You'll weep: your heartstrings are not bound with rigid iron,
　And there's no flint-stone set in your tender heart.
No young man and no young virgin will be able
　To go home with dry eyes from my funeral.
Do no injury to my ghost, but spare your flowing
　Locks, Delia; spare those tender cheeks.
And meanwhile, while the fates allow, let our loves be united;
　Death, with his head shrouded in gloom, will soon arrive;
The age of inactivity creeps up on us, when love will no longer
　　suit us –
　Nor being grey-headed and yet speaking words of blandish-
　　ment.
Now light love must be taken in hand, while there's no inhibition
　Against breaking doors, and while quarreling is still a joy.
On this field I am general, and a soldier born; you, signals and
　　trumpets,
　Keep well away, and take your wounds with you for greedy
　　men.
Take your profits too; happy in the pile I have put together,
　I may look down on riches, and look down on want.

## I.ii

Strengthen the wine, drown these fresh agonies,
　That sleep may overpower my weary eyes;
Let none wake me as Bacchus stuns my brain,
　And my doomed love finds its relief from pain.
My girl is now watched by a cruel guard,
　Her solid door is shut and firmly barred.
You, uncomplaisant keeper's door, may showers
　Lash you, and thunderbolts hurled by Jove's powers.
Swayed by my tears, open for me alone,
　And, as I turn your hinge-post, do not groan.
If I have cursed you in my insanity,
　Forgive it – let the curses fall on me.
Remember now those litany-filled hours,
　When on your posts I hung my wreaths of flowers.

And, Delia, you must boldly trick your guard;
　Venus herself assists those who have dared,
And youths who attempt thresholds not tried before,
　And girls who will unlatch a fast-barred door.
She teaches stealth in creeping out of bed,
　And how to place the feet with noiseless tread,
How one may talk under a husband's eyes
　With nods, and with set signs speak pleasantries –
But not to all – those sloth has not delay'd
　She helps, nor night's thick darkness made afraid.

Roaming the city in distress by night
　I find no harm, protected by her might.

She will let no one meet me with a sword
  To wound, or rob my clothes for his reward.
Once in love's power one may pass anywhere –
  Sacrosanct; ambushes can cause no fear.
The chills of winter night can do no harm;
  I face the soaking showers without alarm;
No hardship – if she unbars the doorway wide,
  Snaps her fingers, and summons me inside.
All people who approach us, spare your eyes;
  It's Venus' will to hide her robberies.
Don't scare us with loud footsteps, or inquire
  Our names, or come close with the torch's fire.
If someone does by chance see, he must hide
  The fact; by all gods it must be denied.
If someone talks he'll find Venus to be
  True child of blood and of the raging sea;
Your husband won't believe him in his heart –
  I learnt this through a witch's magic art.


I've seen her drawing stars down from the sky,
  And turning rapid streams by sorcery;
She splits the soil, and from beneath their stones
  Draws ghosts, and from warm pyres calls bones.
With crooning spells she holds shades from below –
  She sprinkles them with milk, and back they go.
At will she drives the clouds from heaven's grim face,
  Hides summer skies, and calls snow in their place.
She knows Medea's every poisonous herb,
  And Hecat's wild hounds she alone can curb.


She wrote a spell, that you might steal his wit –
  Chant it three times, and after each time spit.

Then he won't credit anything that's said –
   Not his own eyes, that see us both in bed.
Keep clear of others, though; with them he'll find
   The truth; about me only he'll be blind.
Why trust her? She it was said she could free
   My heart from love, by herbs and sorcery.
With fire she cleansed me and by clear moonlight
   A dusky beast fell for the dark god's rite.
It was not for release I made my prayer,
   (I could not), but that you should also care.


He must be a man of iron who could pursue
   Arms and rapine – the fool! – instead of you.
Then let him rout Cilician regiments,
   And on ground won from them dispose his tents;
Let him be wound in silver, sheathed in gold,
   Sit on a swift horse wondrous to behold;
If but with Delia I may yoke my pair,
   And on the old hill feed my flock with her;
While my unwarlike arms enfold her round,
   Softly I'll sleep even on the naked ground.
What use to watch on a rich couch till light,
   If tears of fruitless love outlast the night?
Embroidered rugs and feather beds can't bring
   Us sleep, nor water's drowsy murmuring.


Have words of mine injured great Venus' might,
   And is my tongue now punished for the slight?
Am I accused of entering unpurified
   Or stealing garlands from the altar-side?
If I were guilty I'd fall instantly
   And kiss the temple threshold on my knee,

And crawl prostrate along the precinct floor,
  And beat my head against the holy door.
Beware, you who so gaily mock my fate –
  The god will find new victims soon or late.
I've seen a man who mocked young love's distress
  Bowing, when old, to Venus' stern duress,
In quavering tones composing badinage,
  And trying to prink his hair, now white with age;
He stood outside her door quite undismayed,
  Or in mid-forum stopped her passing maid.
Youths and boys jostle round; and for protection
  Each spits in his young breast to avert the infection.

Venus, be kind; to you my heart is bound;
  Why burn in rage the fruits from your own ground?

## I.iii                    *To Messalla*

You'll sail without me through the Aegean sea;
   I hope you and your staff will think of me.
I'm sick and stuck in strange Phaeacia's land:
   Touch me not, greedy Death, with your black hand.
Touch not, dark Death! No mother here with moans
   May gather to her bosom my charred bones,
No sister here may my burnt ash perfume
   With nard or weep dishevelled by my tomb;
Delia's not here, who asked each shrine, they say,
   For oracles, before I went away.

Thrice she drew lots to see what they would tell;
   Thrice said the acolyte that all was well:
All spelled return; unchecked her tears still flowed,
   With many backward glances at my road.
I cheered her, but when all was set to part,
   Wildly sought reasons to delay my start;
Made birds or ominous words pretexts to stay,
   Or claimed I could not leave on Saturn's day.
I set off, but how often did I see
   In each false step presage of misery.
Venture no partings Cupid has not blessed –
   You'll live to know you've flouted his behest!

What is your Isis, Delia, to me now,
   Or her brass sistrum rattled to and fro,
Your strict observances, the bathing rites,
   And sleeping chastely all those lonely nights?

Help, goddess, help! Your powers to cure we know,
    And painted tablets in your temples show.
Make Delia, as she promised, veiled in gauze
    Sit out her vigils by your holy doors,
And praise you twice a day with hair unbound,
    Conspicuous, as the Egyptians throng around.
Let me again stand at my household shrine,
    With incense for the Lares of my line.


How well they lived in Saturn's time, before
    Ways were disclosed to every distant shore.
The pine tree had not yet scorned the dark seas,
    Or loosed its bellying canvas to the breeze.
The wandering shipman seeking gain abroad
    Had never heaved his foreign wares on board.
The Bull had not yet bowed his neck beneath
    The yoke, nor steeds champed harness with tame teeth.
No dwelling then had doors, no boundary-stone
    Stood on the land to mark out each man's own.
The oaks gave honey; ewes would run to meet
    The carefree farmer, offering him the teat.
No battle-rage was known, nor war's alarms;
    The smith's unfeeling art had not forged arms.


But now Jove rules and bloody wounds are rife,
    Drowning, and countless ways of losing life.
O father, spare me; on my heart no lies
    Hang heavy, no false oaths, or blasphemies.
But if I have lived out my fated time,
    Let there be carved above my bones this rhyme:
*Here lies Tibullus, snatched by Death's cruel hand,*
    *Messalla's follower by sea and land.*

But since I've never scorned the power Love wields,
   Venus shall lead me to the Elysian fields;
There songs and dances reign, and through the sky
   Birds with sweet voices chirrup as they fly.
The earth untilled bears cassia; all around
   Sweet roses flourish in the generous ground.
There ranks of boys mingling with young girls play;
   There wars begun by love are fought all day.
Those whom Death snatched because of love live there
   Wearing proud wreaths of myrtle in their hair.


The home of evil lies in night profound,
   Obscure, with murky rivers circling round.
With waving snakes for locks Tisiphone
   Storms here and there, while the damned spirits flee.
The black dog Cerberus, with snake-ringed jaws,
   Hisses and watches by the brazen doors.
Bound on his whirling wheel Ixion spins –
   Juno's assaulter punished for his sins.
Tityos, across nine acres stretched, regales
   The tireless vultures with his black entrails.
Tantalus stands in water, plagued by thirst –
   He bends – but finds the pools have now dispersed.
For slighting Venus' powers Danaus' daughters
   Draw for their leaking vessels Lethe's waters.
This is the place for that man who profanes
   My love, or wishes on me long campaigns.


Delia, be true; some chaperone sit by,
   And zealously protect your chastity;
She can tell stories, and by lamplight pull
   The long thread from the distaff's store of wool;

Tied to their weary tasks the maids sit round,
  And, growing sleepy, drop them to the ground.
Then I'll burst in quite unexpectedly,
  Seeming a god sent to you from the sky.
Then rise, just as you are, with hair untied,
  And run, my Delia, barefoot to my side.

Soon may pale Dawn's pink steeds bring us, I pray,
  The morning star that heralds such a day.

## I.iv

'O Priapus, shade and shelter be yours,
   That sun and snow may never harm your head –
What is your trick for captivating lovely boys?
   After all your beard's not oiled and your hair uncombed.
You measure out the long frost of winter naked,
   And in nakedness the dry season of the summer dog-star.'
So I spoke, and Bacchus' earthy son,
   Armed with his curving sickle, gave me this response:

'Avoid them; don't let yourself near a gang of blooming
      boys;
   In every one of them there'll be some valid ground for passion.
One boy is delightful for his tight rein on a horse,
   Another parts still water with a chest as white as snow;
One captivates you with his bold effrontery; another boy's
   Soft cheeks have virgin modesty standing guard.
Even if at first he does refuse, don't you give in
   Through lack of perseverance; he'll soon accept the yoke.
Time teaches lions to obey mankind,
   Time eats away the solid rock with feeble water.
The year matures the grapes on sunny hillsides,
   The year brings round the stars in an unchanging sequence.
Don't hesitate to swear; the winds sweep off false oaths of love
   Across the land and wavetops into nothingness.
Praise be to Jupiter – the Father decreed they had no force,
   If sworn in desire by misplaced love.
Dictynna overlooks the protestations you make by her arrows;
   Likewise Minerva with her locks.

72

Slowness is the only thing that will undo you; how fast
  Youth passes; days don't stand idle, don't come back.
How quickly earth is done with her bright pigments;
  How quickly the high poplar's finished with her lovely tresses.
How low lies he, when weak senility's decree comes upon him,
  The horse that once shot from the Elean starting-gate.
Many a man I've seen, when age pressed hard,
  Groaning for the folly of his vanished days.
The cruel gods! Snakes may shed the years and be renewed,
  But fate has granted no reprieve for beauty.
Only Bacchus and Apollo have eternal youth,
  Their uncropped hair their glorious due.
You now, give in to your young man's every whim;
  Love wins a million victories by pandering.
Agree to go with him, however long a road he contemplates,
  Even when the dog-star grills the fields with baking thirst;
Even if the rainbow stripes the dark sky with iridescent streaks,
  Threatening the coming downpour;
Or if he intends to pass on shipboard through the inky waves,
  Seize oars and urge the boat through the sea yourself;
Have no regret for unremitting toil endured,
  Or hands worn down with unaccustomed tasks;
If his desire is to hem high valleys with his snares,
  And you can please him by it, shoulder cheerfully the nets.
If fencing's what he wants, then limber up your arm and take
      him on;
  Occasionally presenting him your open flank, so he can win.
Then he'll be kind, then you can grasp
  The precious kiss; he will resist, but snatch and you'll have it.
At first you'll have to snatch; later you'll only have to ask;
  And finally he'll embrace you at his own desire.
Unfortunately our age has grown used to some miserable prac-
      tices –

Nowadays a tender young boy will expect a present.
A malevolent stone lie heavy on your bones,
    You, who first introduced to men the sale of love.
Give your heart where the Muses are, boys; love learned poets;
    Golden gifts should not outshine the damsels of Pierus.
Through poetry Nisus' lock is purple yet; if there were none,
    The ivory never would have gleamed from Pelops' shoulder.
Supported by the Muses, a man shall live as long as earth breeds
        oaks,
    The sky its stars, and rivers water.
If he is deaf to them and sells his affections,
    Then let him follow Ops of Ida's chariots,
Count up three hundred cities in his wanderings,
    And finally slash off his scorned member to the Phrygian
        music.
Venus indeed wills that we should woo our loves,
    And takes the part of doleful entreaties and lovelorn tears.'

So pronounced the god – for me to recite to Titius;
    But Titius' wife won't let him recall my words for an instant.
In his case he can obey her, if he must; but you, maltreated of
        some sly, sophisticated boy,
    You must make of me your well-attended schoolmaster.
Each man has his point of pride – I stand to be consultant
    To scorned lovers; my door is open to you all.
I'll see the day, when, as I bear the torch of Venus' precepts,
    Old as I am, my young supporters shall chair me home.
But oh, how lingering the tortures Marathus inflicts;
    My techniques, my subterfuges are not quite enough.
Spare me I beg you, boy, lest I become a cautionary tale,
    And people titter at my useless pedantry.

# I.v

I had my hackles up and talked about bearing divorce with ease;
  But this brave glorious mood is now a long way off.
I'm driven like a whipped top over the flat spaces,
  Steered by a quick boy with an art long practis'd.
Brand the wild beast I was and rack him, to check in future
  Any fancy for grand talk; break in his bristling words.
To me as I am show mercy, by the treaty of our secret bed, I beg
      you,
  By the love we made and our two heads side by side.

For when you lay worn out by that demoralizing sickness,
  I was the one that saved you with my prayers;
I was the one to scatter clean sulphur round you,
  After the crone had chanted the preliminary spells;
I took care of your cruel dreams for you, to pre-empt their
      mischief,
  Three times, as due, appeasing them with consecrated flour;
In woollen fillets and loose robes nine times I gave
  At dead of night the promised offerings to Trivia.
Yes, I did everything required: and someone else enjoys my love
  And happily reaps the profits of my prayers.
And yet, if you were to be spared, I pictured a life
  Of bliss; but I was a fool – gods shook their heads.

*I'll cultivate my farm*, I said, *and Delia will be there to guard the
      produce;
  While in the blazing sun the threshing-floor treads out the
      harvest;*

*Or else she'll watch the bunches in the brimful troughs*
  *And the glistening must forced down by flying feet;*
*She'll grow used to counting flocks; the slave-child too will learn*
  *To play chattering in his loving mistress' lap;*
*She'll come to know the offerings to make to the farm-gods - grapes*
      *for the vine,*
  *Corn-ears for the harvest, and a hot-pot for the flock.*
*Let her be mistress of the farmhands, let them be her concern -*
  *My delight but to be a nobody in the house!*
*And Messalla shall arrive - for Delia to pull down for him*
  *Sweet fruit from the choicest trees,*
*And, respecting such glory, sedulously look to his needs,*
  *Prepare his dishes, and wait on him in person.*
Such was my fantasy. Now East and South winds take my
      prayers
  And toss them the length of perfumed Armenia.


Many times have I tried banishing care with drink,
  But pain had turned all my wine to tears.
Many times I've clutched another girl; but at the approach to joy
  Venus reminded me of Her and abandoned me.
Then, as she left, the girl would say I was entranced,
  And in her shame tell me my mistress knew the occult arts.
But this effect is not achieved by spells - her face and soft arms
  Are enough for my girl to bind me with, and that golden hair.
*Such was the Nereid who to Haemonian Peleus once*
  *Rode dark and gleaming on a bridled fish - Thetis.*
These are the charms that undid me. And now a rich lover
  Is at her side - the skilful bawd has made a set at me for my
      destruction.


*Blood-drenched food may she eat, and with a gory mouth*
  *Drink dismal cups heavily diluted - with gall;*

*Let ghosts flit round her perpetually bemoaning*
  *Their fate, and let the violent vampire screech from the rooftops.*
*Goaded crazy by hunger let her search for weeds on graves*
  *And bones abandoned by the savage wolves;*
*Let her run with naked belly screaming through the cities*
  *Driven from the crossways by a snapping herd of dogs.*
*It shall be so; a god portends it: a lover has guardian powers,*
  *And Venus, abandoned for a lawless bond, grows cruel.*


Abandon, as soon as may be, the grasping wise-woman's teach-
        ing;
  All love is crushed when it is bought with gifts.
*A poor man will always be by you; he will be first*
  *To reach you, and cling fast to your vulnerable side;*
*A poor man, reliable escort in the jostling crowds,*
  *Will give his arm for you to lean on and make a way.*
*A poor man can take you undetected to your secret friends*
  *And himself pull off the sandals from your snow-white feet.*


But these verses are idle, and her door opens not for words,
  But must be knocked at with crammed knuckles.
And you, preferred as of now, beware the fate I suffer;
  Swift is the rim of the wheel that fickle Fortune turns on –
It's no accident that a man is this moment standing by the door,
  Full of perseverance – looking in front of him and then with-
        drawing,
Pretending to pass the house, and then, when he's alone, return-
        ing –
  Constantly clearing his throat on the threshold.
Some secret love has plans for itself. So, enjoy her, won't you,
  While you can; your boat sails on as yet unruffled waters.

## I.vi

Always, for my inducement, smiling is the face you show,
    Thereafter to a wretched lover frowning and harsh, O Love!
What am I to you, heartless being? Is it so much to boast of
    For a god – to have laid snares for a mortal?
Spread indeed for me is the net; this moment, furtively,
    My skilful Delia warms some man in the quiet of night.
Indeed she denies, on oath, but it's hard to believe her,
    When to her husband she persists in denying me.
Unfortunately I was the one who taught her how to make fools
    Of guards – now put down, alas! by my own technique!
The next thing was she learned to create reasons for sleeping
        alone,
    And after that how doors could be made to pivot noiselessly.
Subsequently I gave her herbs and extracts with which to make
        marks vanish –
    Marks made by love with the mutual print of teeth.

And you, incautious husband of this deceiving girl,
    See that my interests too are protected – see to it that she does
        not stray at all;
Take care that she doesn't frequent the company and talk of
        youths,
    Or recline with her robe loose and her breasts revealed,
Or nod behind your back, or with a finger spread spilled wine
    And trace marks on the round top of the table;
Tremble as often as she leaves the house, even if she claims to be
        visiting
    The rites of the Bona Dea prohibited for males.

If you would trust her to me, I'd follow her alone as far as the
    altar,
  My eyes fixed where I'd have no fear for their blinding.
Many a time I have deliberately touched her hand,
  Pretending to appraise a jewel or a ring.
Often I have procured sleep for you, while I was drinking
  Triumphant cups of sobriety – of water instead of wine.
I did not hurt you maliciously; I confess, but pardon me;
  Love told me to; who could bear arms against a god?
I was the one, now not too shy to speak the truth,
  Whom your dog was menacing all night long.
What use have you for a tender wife? If you can't protect your
    own,
  It makes no difference that the key's turned in the lock.
It's you she holds, but other absent loves she sighs for –
  And unexpectedly complains she has a headache!
You should entrust her to me; I do not shrink from the cruel
    lashes
  Of a mistress, nor reject the shackles for my feet.
You'd best keep clear then, all you who cultivate your hair
  And wear your togas flowing down in fluted folds.
And if you meet us, avoid any accusations;
  Pass by on the other side, or take another road.


A god himself orders this done – so prophesied
  The great priestess to me with god-sent utterance;
Who, when tossed by Bellona's urge, fears neither biting
  Flame nor plaited lashes in her ecstasy.
She hacks her own arms violently with her axe
  And with the splashing blood sprinkles the goddess un-
    punished –
Stands pierced in her side with the spit, stands wounded in her
    breast,

And rhymes on the things to come that the great goddess puts
      into her mind:
*Be careful how you do mischief to a girl Love guards,*
    *Or you may regret learning this lesson later at great cost.*
*Touch her – your wealth seeps away like the blood from my wound,*
    *And as this ash is plundered by the winds.*
And she named some punishment in your case, my Delia;
    If you should incur the blame, I hope she is lenient.


It's not for your sake, though, that I wish you mercy,
    But your mother moves me and quells my anger – old lady of
      pure gold.
She brings me to you in the dark and with much trembling
    Silently and secretly joins our hands together.
At night she awaits me, pressed to the door, and far off
    She knows the clatter of my feet as I approach.
Live long for me, sweet old lady: I'd share with you
    My own years, if it were sanctioned, to add them to yours.
On your account alone I'll always love you and your daughter;
    Whatever she does, her blood at any rate is yours.
Let her forget her promiscuity, tell her, even though no veil
    Nets up her hair and no long robe impedes her feet.
The terms for me may be as hard: not to praise any woman
    Without her flying at my eyeballs;
And if she thinks I've gone astray, even though I don't deserve
    it,
    I may be dragged out by the hair and thrown flat in the street.
I'd never want to strike at Delia, but if such madness came on
    me,
    I'd willingly forego the possession of my hands.
And yet avoid promiscuousness through trust, not the stern
    grip of fear;
    Let love that you share with me keep you for me in my absence.

The girl who was true to nobody, when overwhelmed by age
  In her decrepitude shall draw with shaking hand the twisted
      strands,
And tie the firm-spun threads to looms on contract,
  And bleach the tufts pulled from the snowy fleece.
The companies of youths see this with a contented heart,
  Repeating that her age deserves to undergo these many hard-
      ships.
Venus looks at her weeping from the peak of high Olympus,
  And warns us of the bitterness that waits for treachery.

But these are curses that I wish for others; in our case, Delia,
  As our hair grows grey, let us still be textbooks of true love.

## I.vii

This day the Fates foretold, spinning the threads
    Of Destiny that no god can unwind;
A man should live, to rout the Aquitanian tribes,
    And cow the Aude, conquered by his brave troops.
It's happened; the Roman youth have seen new triumphs,
    And leaders with their captured wrists in fetters.
You, Messalla, an ivory chariot with white horses
    Carried crowned with the victor's laurel.

I shared in these honours, as will witness the Pyrenees
    By the Adour, and the shore of Ocean in Saintonge,
And Saône, and rapid Rhone, and wide Garonne, and Loire,
    The dark water of the flaxen-haired Carnutes;
Or should I mention Cydnus, with silent ripples creeping
    Smooth, blue-black and calm through the lagoon?
Or great Taurus, head in the sky, touching the clouds,
    Cold nurse of the long-haired Cilicians?
Or the white dove, sacred to the Palestinian,
    That flits inviolate from town to town?
Or Tyre, gazing out at the vast sea from her towers,
    That first learnt how to trust a ship to winds?
Or fertile Nile, whose waters flood in summer,
    While Sirius cracks the dry-baked fields?

Father Nile, what is the reason that you hide
    Your spring – in what land can I say it lurks?
Your country begs no showers, no dry grass there
    Prays to the rain-god – and you are the cause.

The barbarous youth, brought up to mourn the ox of Memphis
    Extol and worship you as their own Osiris.

It was Osiris' skilful hand formed the first plough,
    First harried the unresisting earth with iron,
First confidently buried seeds in virgin soil,
    First picked the fruits from trees they did not recognize;
He taught us how to tie young vines to stakes,
    And prune their green crowns with the hard-edged hook;
The ripe bunches, pressed by primitive feet,
    Produced their delightful flavours first for him.
That was the juice that taught us how to intune our voices,
    And jerked our ignorant arms and legs in rhythm;
And when the farmer's heart is weary with long labour
    The wine-god makes him glad and brings release.
The wine-god brings rest to mankind in misery,
    Though their legs clank with iron shackles.
Grief and despondency were not meant for you, Osiris,
    But dancing and singing and lighthearted love;
Coloured bouquets, and foreheads twined with ivy,
    And saffron tunics flowing down to soft young feet;
And purple robes and sweetly singing flutes,
    And little baskets with their ritual secrets.

Come with a hundred reels and dances; honour with us
    The guardian-spirit; bathe his forehead in wine.
Let perfumes bead with drops his glistening hair;
    Garland his head and neck with delicate wreaths.
Come, guardian, like this to us today, and I will bring
    Meal-cakes sweetened with King Mopsopus' honey.
To Messalla's progeny bring increase; let them multiply
    His deeds, and gather round to bring respect to his old
        age.

And the man detained in Tusculum or ancient gleaming Alba
  Must testify to the road that he has bequeathed.
For there, by his bounty, hard concrete has been laid;
  There with careful skill the granite blocks are jointed.
And when from the great city the farmer comes home late
  And does not stumble, he'll sing Messalla's praise.

And you, birthday-spirit, to be hymned for many years,
  Come, and shine on us with brighter and ever brighter face.

I.viii  *To Pholoe*

The sense of lovers' nods no one can hide
  From me, nor what their light soft words betide.
No lots, no entrails showed the Fates to me,
  No birdsong gave me note of things to be.
Venus, with many a lash, my arms entwined
  In magic knots, has well tutored my mind.
Do not pretend; the god galls harder still
  Those that he sees succumb against their will.
What good can combing your soft hair procure,
  What use these frequent changes of coiffure?
To improve your cheeks with rouge little avails,
  Or to hire an artist's hand to trim your nails.
Changing your robes and mantles is no use,
  Nor squeezing both feet tightly in the noose.
Your rival pleases, though her face and hair
  Don't show the patient use of skill and care.
Has some old woman put a spell on you
  At dead of night, or charmed you with her brew?
Spells draw from nearby fields a neighbour's crops;
  At sound of them the angry serpent stops;
They would pull from her car by incantations
  The moon – but for the gongs' reverberations.
But why complain that this downfall was laid
  By spells or herbs? Beauty needs no such aid;
The touch of flesh, kisses' long ecstasy –
  These do the harm – and twining thigh in thigh.
Do not be hard for your young man to win;
  Venus will punish such a heinous sin.

Don't ask for gifts – they're for grey heads to give,
    That their cold limbs may in soft arms revive.
Dearer than gold a boy of smooth white face,
    And no rough beard to chafe your long embrace.
Give him your gleaming arms for his support,
    And kings' great riches may be set at nought.
Venus will see you bring the boy to bed,
    Pressing close to your breast in bashful dread,
Grant kisses to wet tongues that fight for breath,
    And help you print his neck with marks of teeth.
The girl who sleeps unloved, cold and alone,
    Finds little joy in any precious stone.
Too late is love recalled, and youth, now dead –
    Too late – when white old age has bleached the head.
Then looks are thought of, then the hair must hide
    Its years, with the green husk of walnuts dyed.
Then we take pains to prune each silver thread,
    And wear a new face where the old is shed.
While still you see your life's first flowering day,
    Use it; with speedy steps it glides away.
Don't torture him; what glory can it hold
    To rout a boy? Be hard but to the old.
Spare the green youth; he knows no taint of blame,
    But too much love has sallowed his whole frame.
*Be kind*, he says; *a watch may be defeated;*
    *Love grants to lovers that guards may be cheated.*
*I am well versed in stealing all Love's blisses –*
    *Soft breathing, and the silent theft of kisses.*
*Even at dead of night I can steal round*
    *And unlock bolted doors without a sound.*
*But if she scorns her boy, what use this skill;*
    *Or runs from bed, to please her cruel will?*

*Or having promised, leaves me all alone,*
  *And I must lie awake with many a groan?*
*Dreaming she'll come, whatever sound I hear*
  *I take to be her footstep coming near.*
Weep no more, boy; her heart cannot be tamed.
  Your eyes are puffed with weeping and inflamed.
I warn you, girl, the gods hate haughtiness;
  The incense that you burn is profitless.
This boy once laughed at wretched lovers' kind,
  Not seeing the god of vengeance close behind.
He often mocked at tears of pain, they say,
  And checked an eager love with feigned delay.
Now he can't bear to be held at a distance,
  And hates to meet the barred door's stern resistance.
But punishment, my girl, awaits disdain;
  How much you'll long to live this day again!

I.ix                    *To Marathus*

Why, being then set to wrong my helpless love,
    Swear, but to break them, oaths by heaven above?
Poor wretch, though at first you hide your perjury,
    At last comes vengeance treading silently.
Spare him, you gods – the beautiful may be
    Just once allowed to scorn your power scotfree.
For gain the ploughman yokes bulls to the plough
    And leans their labour on the soil below.
The stars across the wind-obeying main
    Guide surely the unsure vessels – seeking gain.
My boy has been ensnared by gifts – gods turn
    All gifts to water which they do not burn.
But soon he'll pay the price; dust will not spare
    His glamour, winds will make coarse his sleek hair,
His face be tanned, bleached by the sun his head,
    His tender feet with long roads chafed and red.
How often have I urged '*Don't smirch that grace*
    *With gold; harm hides behind gold's glinting face.*
*If some, ensnared by wealth, have outraged love,*
    *Venus is harsh to such, and hard to move.*
*Rather than this engulf with flames this head:*
    *Stab me and cut my back with whips instead.*
*Don't hope your planned misdeeds can stay concealed;*
    *Gods know, and leave no treachery unrevealed.*
*A safe accomplice, by the gods' design,*
    *Has often freely talked when drunk with wine.*
*Gods have made tongues give utterance unbidden,*
    *Even in sleep, and tell of things best hidden.'*

So did I speak; but now it wounds my pride
   That I fell at your tender feet and cried.
Then would you swear that for no weight of gold
   Or gems would your true faith ever be sold.
Not if Campania could thus be got,
   Or the Falernian field, the wine-god's plot.
You'd make me think, with such deceiving skill,
   That stars don't shine and rivers run uphill.
You even wept: unschooled like you to lie
   I'd fondly wipe your cheeks' moist channels dry.

What could I do – but that you suffered too?
   May your girl's heart prove light, so taught by you.
To keep eavesdroppers from your talk at night,
   I've often stood outside holding a light.
Often she's come, when I took up your cause,
   Unhoped for, hiding veiled behind closed doors.
I wrecked my hopes, so trusting, so obtuse;
   I might have been more wary of your noose.
I wrote moonstruck verses of adulation –
   Now blushing for that Muse's inspiration.
May Vulcan scorch the lines with shrivelling flames,
   And rivers destroy them in their flowing streams.
Curse you, whose aim is but to sell your charms
   And win fat recompense in brimful palms,
And you who dared corrupt the boy with gifts –
   May your wife ever mock you with her shifts,
And when she's tired her lover out unseen,
   Lie with you spent – a blanket in between;
Your bed bear strange marks for you to discover,
   Your house be open to each greedy lover;
Let her surpass her wanton sister's list
   Of cups downed, and of men drained and dismissed;

She draws her drinking out till dawn, they say;
   Until the daystar's wheel heralds the day;
No one knows better how to waste the night,
   Or play the variations till the light;
And your wife's learnt them all; and you don't see
   She moves her limbs with a new artistry.
Do you suppose she draws the toothed comb through
   Those locks, and prinks them up, for you?
Does she walk out because of your fair charms
   In Tyrian drapes, with gold bands on her arms?
No – but she wants to attract a young man's eye,
   For whom she'd damn your house and property –
Not from depravity, but to escape
   From gouty limbs and from an old man's rape!
And yet with him my boy has passed the night –
   He'd even act a wild beast's catamite.
You dared to sell caresses owed to me,
   And pass my kisses round promiscuously.
You'll weep when I'm held in another's chains,
   Wielding his proud rod over your domains;
And I'll be glad; a golden palm set up
   For Venus shall attest my flowing cup:
*Freed from false love Tibullus offers this,*
   *And begs you think of him with gratefulness.*

I.x

Who first introduced the terrible sword?
  What a brute he was, truly a brute-steel-hearted man!
From then on murder was hereditary in man, and war was born,
  The shorter way was opened to the terror of death.
Or is the man innocent, to be pitied rather, we being the ones
    Who turn what he designed against wild beasts to our own
      misfortunes?
This is surely the fault of precious gold; there were no wars,
    When the cup that stood ready for the feast was made of
      beechwood.
There were no strongholds then, no pales; the shepherd looked
      for sleep
  Among his piebald flocks in peace of mind.
If I had lived in those days, I would not have known the crowd's
      desperate weapons,
  Or heard with quivering heart the trumpet-call.
But as it is I'm pulled off to war, and some enemy soldier per-
      haps has on his back
  Spears that are destined to come to rest in my side.

Preserve me, gods of my father's house: it was you that fed me
      before,
  When as a green young boy I used to race around your feet.
Feel no shame to be made from ancient tree-stumps:
  You inhabited my ancestor's house in such a form.
They kept better faith in those days, when with inexpensive
      ceremony
  The gods of wood stood in their tiny shrine.

They were appeased enough by the first fruits of a bunch of
    grapes,
  Or the dedication of a wreath of bearded wheat-ears.
A man whose prayer was answered brought his barley-cakes
  And at his heels his small daughter brought an untouched
    honeycomb.
So drive the javelins away from me you family gods,
  And you, my country piglet picked from the full sty for the
    sacrifice;
Behind you I shall follow in a clean robe carrying baskets
  Twined with myrtle, with myrtle round my own head too.
This is the way I would find favour with you; another can be
    brave in war,
  And wafted by Mars lay low the chieftains of the enemy,
And then return from the war and tell me his story over a drink,
  Sketching the camp in wine on the table top.

How mad – actually to fetch black Death to the battle!
  He hangs over us as it is and creeps up on us with silent tread.
There are no crops below, no vineyards – only aggressive
  Cerberus, and the ugly boatman of the Stygian stream;
There with gouged cheeks and charred hair
  The ghost-white crowd swirls by the darkened lakes.

How much more laudable to get your family
  And let old age creep over you in your cottage.
The master follows his sheep, his son the lambs,
  His wife prepares warm water for him when he's tired.
That's the life for me – to let my head get steadily whiter,
  And as an old man call to mind the actions of the past.
And meanwhile Peace shall farm my fields. Fair Peace in the
    beginning
  Led oxen under the curving yoke to plough;

Peace dunged the vines and stored the grape-juice
    For the father's jar to pour the wine out to the son;
In Peace the fork and ploughshare shine; in a dark corner
    Rust seizes on the tough soldier's unsmiling arms;
And out of the grove the countryman, not a little drunk,
    Drives home his wife and progeny in the cart.

Then the war of love grows warm, a woman's hair is torn,
    Her door is broken in, and she grows plaintive;
Bruised on her tender cheeks she sheds tears; while the victor
        sobs too
    That his crazy hands should have been so violent;
And Cupid, the mischief-maker, feeds the quarrel with insults,
    And sits inflexibly between the angry couple.
How stony-hearted, how iron-hard to beat one's girl;
    Such a man dethrones the gods in heaven.
Enough to rip the thin garment from her body,
    And ruin the elaborate structure of her hair,
Enough to call out her tears; and four times happy
    The man who brings his gentle girl to weep by sulking.
But to be physically rough – he ought to be wearing the shield
        and stakes
    And put a long long distance between himself and Venus.

But as for me, kind Peace, come and possess my ears of wheat,
    And from your white bosom overflow with fruit.

# BOOK TWO
## TIBULLUS

## II.i

All present, keep holy silence; we cleanse the fields and the
          harvest,
  To re-enact the ceremony our fathers handed down.
Come Bacchus, and down from your horns let there be dangled
  Sweet grapes, and, Ceres, bind your forehead with ears.
Let there be rest for the ground this holy morning, rest too for
          the ploughman;
  Let the hard labour stop, and hang up the share.
Untie the traces from the yokes: the bullocks must now stand
          idle
  By full mangers, with garlands on their heads.
All work that is done be for the god; let none of the women
  Dare to lay her spinner's hand on her portion of wool.
You too must not be near us, must now draw away from the
          altar,
  You, to whom Venus brought her joys last night.
Gods love what is pure and devoted: come then with clean
          clothing
  And take the spring water up in clean-washed hands.
See how the dedicated lamb goes to the resplendent altars,
  And the white-robed company, hair tied behind with olive-
          sprigs.
Gods of the land, we purify the fields, we purify the farmers;
  Drive evil away from our borders, O you gods,
That the crop shall not mock the harvest with cheating grasses,
  Nor the loping wolves terrify the slower lamb.
Then shall the farmer, face shining, and confident in full furrows
  Pile up the broad logs on the glowing fire,

And the slave-born children, good sign of a well-filled settler,
    Will play in gangs and build lath-shelters by the fire.
I pray for things that shall be – look there at the good omens in
        the entrails;
    See how the filament proclaims the gods are mild.
Bring out for me now the smoked Falernian from that far distant
    Consulship, and untie the bonds of a Chian jar.
Let wine make a festival of today; on a feast-day there's no reason
    To blush at being drunk and mismanaging one's crazy steps.
But each of us must call Messalla's health over each cupful,
    And individual voices sound his absent name.
Messalla, on everyone's lips for your Aquitanian triumph,
    And in your victory shedding lustre on your bearded sires,
Draw near and inspire me with your breath, while in these verses
    Due thanks is paid to the heavenly tillers of the soil.
I write of farms and the gods of the country. Under their guid-
        ance
    Man's life was once taught to drive away hunger with acorns
        from oaks;
They first showed him how to put small planks together
    And roof his tiny homes with green leaves.
These men were the first to school bulls, tradition tells us,
    To servitude, and fix wheels under their carts.
Their wild ways of feeding left them, the apple-tree was planted,
    The fertile garden drank the irrigating streams.
Compressed by feet the gold grape-bunches offered their juices,
    And sober water was mixed with carefree wine.
The farms produce their harvests when, in the heat of the dog-
        star,
    The yearling land lays up its yellow locks.
In the country the bee piles up light flowers in his hive of the
        springtime,
    So that by his untiring efforts sweet honey may fill the combs.

It was a farmer, glutted with his incessant ploughing,
  Who first sang country words to a stated rhythm,
And when replete first played a tune on a pipe of dry oatstraw,
    So he might sing the praise of the gods his own craft had
      shaped.
And it was a farmer, stained with blushing cinnabar, O Bacchus,
  Who from his still tentative skill first led the dance.
Later a he-goat, given from a full sheepfold as a prize fit to
    remember,
  A leader for his flock, increased his stunted wealth.
It was on a farm in spring that a slave first made a wreath of
    blossoms
  And laid it up for the ancient household gods.
On farms too, one day to engage attentiveness in young females,
  The gleaming sheep wears the soft fleece on his back.
From here comes woman's work – distaffs and portions;
  Hence too the spindle at thumb's touch spins the task;
And some weaver, tirelessly involved in the work of Minerva,
  Sings, and the loom rattles as the warp-weights clash.
Cupid himself was born in the fields and amongst the cattle,
  So runs the legend, and surrounded by untamed mares.
It was there he first practised with his unskilled bow and arrows.
  Poor me! How skilful are the hands he has now!
No longer does he aim at the cattle as before; now it's his passion
  To transfix girls and tame the spirit of bold young men.
He has robbed young men of their wealth, and in old age made
    them utter
  By the door of an angry woman words full of shame.
Led by him, girls quietly step over sleeping watchmen
  And make their way to their lovers alone in the dark,
And test the way ahead with their feet on the hook of excite-
    ment,
  While their hands grope for the blinded path ahead.

Pitiable the fate of those that this god presses hard on; and happy
　　The man on whom a calm Love gently breathes.
Dedicated boy, come to our festal banquet, but lay down your
　　　　arrows
　　And hide far off, I beg you, your blazing brands.
You farmers, sing to this much-venerated god, and call him
　　To your herd; publicly to the herd, and privately each to him-
　　　　self;
Or even summon him out loud: for the noise of the gay crowd's
　　　　laughter
　　Strikes my ears, and the curved flute's Phrygian wail.
Make merry; now Night yokes her horses, and behind their
　　　　mother's chariot
　　The golden Stars follow in abandoned dance,
And last, enfolded in dusky wings and moving in silence,
　　Comes Sleep, and black Dreams on tottering steps.

## II.ii

We must speak words of good omen; Natalis is coming to the
          altar:
   All present, men and women, be careful what you say.
Burn the due incense on the hearth; burn the perfumes
   The gentle Arab sends from his rich land.
Guardian-spirit draw near, and look on at your own ceremonies;
   Soft wreaths adorn our heads for him and sanctify us,
Pure spikenard drip from his temples,
   Fill him with honeycake and satisfy him with wine.
Any request you make of him, Cornutus, be granted;
   Come, why hesitate? He nods in approbation – ask!
I prophesy you will be asking for the loyal love of your wife;
   I think the gods on their part already know your mind;
So don't be thinking after all the arable land of the world,
   That the stout farmer and his sturdy oxen plough,
Or all the jewels the prosperous Indies bring to light,
   Where the wave of the eastern sea glows red –
These prayers will fail; only pray that with pinions fluttering
   Love may fly to you and throw his golden chains around your
          marriage –
Chains to endure for ever until slow age
   Brings on his wrinkles and dyes your hair.
Send us a prosperous omen for this, Natalis, and bless him with
          children,
   And a new young brood play round about your feet.

II.iii                     *To Cornutus*

My girl is staying at someone's country home:
  Only a man of steel could stop in Rome.
Venus now takes a country holiday
  And Cupid learns to talk the ploughmen's way.
At sight of her how vigorously I'd throw
  The rich soil over with my sturdy hoe,
Follow the curved plough like a farmer born,
  While oxen cleft the fields to take the corn;
Nor moan because the sun burnt my thin arms
  And bursting blisters hurt my tender palms.

Even Apollo in Admetus' byre
  Fed bulls, unhelped by unshorn locks or lyre.
He could not cure with herbs his troubled heart
  For Love had overwhelmed his healing art.
He would drive cows to pasture from their shed,
  And bring them home again when they were fed;
Showed men how to put rennet in fresh cream
  And in an instant curdle the white stream.
Then from light reeds they wove baskets for cheese,
  The whey escaping through the interstices.
His sister used to blush, when on the farm
  She met him with a calf held in his arm.
The rude ox, while he sang in some deep dale,
  Would low, and rupture the poetic tale.
Leaders in trouble sought his prophets' aid,
  But had to leave when no reply was made.

His hair, which even Juno wondered at,
  Made Leto grieve to see its unkempt state;
Whoever saw his bare locks hanging down
  Would ask indeed where was Apollo's crown.
Where is your Delos now and Delphic shrine?
  Humble the house Love bids you dwell within.
Happy the days when gods would openly,
  Without shame, own to Venus' mastery.
Now he's a byword; better so for one
  Who loves a girl than be a god – alone.

And as for you, whom Cupid's frown commands
  Make war with me, *beware of wealth and lands*.
This age – true Age of Iron – can but approve
  Of ill-begotten booty, not of love.
Booty has armed hosts warring with fierce breath;
  Hence blood, murder, and shorter roads to death.
Booty made sea-risks double, when it gave
  Rams to the ships tossed by the fickle wave.
Freebooters long to grasp the boundless plain,
  With countless sheep to crop the wide terrain.
Rare stone's the craze – and through the city's hum
  A thousand sturdy teams convey each drum.
The sea is closed by piers – the fish forgets,
  Inside, the untamed ocean's winter threats.
For me, let Samian jars extend my meal,
  Or slippery clay, moulded on Cumae's wheel.
But ah! I see that riches make girls gay.
  If Love likes wealth – let the spoils come my way!
Let Nemesis float in my finery
  And with my gifts catch the whole city's eye.
Let her wear silks made on a loom in Cos
  With lines of golden thread woven across.

Let her have slaves burned brown by India's skies,
   And those the nearing sun-god's chariot dyes.
Let lands compete to colour her attire –
   Crimson from Africa, purple from Tyre.

But him we see enthroned whose gypsumed feet
   Once trod the platform in some foreign street.
You fields of his, that stole my girl from town,
   May Earth hold back the investment in you sown;
And gentle Bacchus, planter of the grape,
   Desert the vats I now curse for her rape.
The dull fields hide such beauty at a price:
   Your vintage is not worth such sacrifice.
If girls will stay in town, then we can spare
   Our crops – revert to our primeval fare.

Our sires ate acorns – Love was theirs at will;
   What loss to have no furrows then to fill.
To those Love breathed on Venus openly
   Gave joy in valleys' cool opacity.
There were no guards, no doors to exclude in pain
   Sad lovers: days of old, return again!
If it were right to see again such times,
   Let the rough skins conceal our shaggy limbs;
If my girl's locked up and access is rare,
   What use are flowing togas as things are?

Take me! I'll plough the fields at my love's nod,
   And not withhold myself from chain and rod.

## II.iv

Slavery confronts me now, and a mistress –
  Farewell, my inheritance, Liberty!
Worse! Slavery unrelieved, and chains:
  Love never eases his victims' bonds;
He burns them, innocent or guilty;
  Remove the firebrands, cruel girl; I am in flames.
To be free from the sensation of such pain,
  How preferable to be a stone on a frozen mountain,
Or as a cliff, to bear the brunt of the raging gales,
  Pounded by the shipwrecking breakers of the ocean.
Now my day is bitter, and the night shade bitterer;
  All times of day are soured with gall.
My verse and its author Apollo are no use to me;
  She's there demanding at all times, with hands cupped.
Keep away, Muses, if you're useless to a lover;
  I do not worship you for the celebration of war,
Or to talk of sun's courses or the nature of the moon,
  When her back-turned chariot retraces its completed cycle.
I only look through poetry for access to my mistress;
  Keep away, Muses, if your themes are powerless.
I must get gifts for her by crime and murder,
  Or else lie weeping outside her bolted house;
Or steal the decorations hung in holy shrines –
  Yes, and I must desecrate Venus above all others –
She is behind the evil deed, and is responsible
  For my rapacious mistress: she must feel my sacrilegious hands.
Damnation take those who collect green emeralds,
  And dye the snow-white sheep in Tyrian purple;

Coan dresses, and the Red Sea's iridescent shell
 Only give girls another cause for greed.
These have corrupted them: hence keys in doors
 And the watchdogs at the entrance.
If you bring a fat bribe, the guard is won,
 The bolts don't bar the way, the dogs don't bark.
Whoever gave the lustful goddess beauty
 Brought a great good among a thousand evils!
So sobs and arguments ring out; from this prime cause
 Love goes into the world an ill-famed vagabond.
Fire and the whirlwind sweep off your hoarded gains,
 For shutting lovers out who cannot find your price.
I hope there'll be men to smile when they see that fire,
 And no busy hand to pour water on the flame.
Death will come, and there will be none to mourn,
 Or make his offering towards your sorry funeral:
Whereas the good, ungrasping girl, if she lives to a hundred,
 Will be mourned with tears beside her burning pyre,
And some old fellow in respect for his past love
 Will throw a wreath on her mound each year,
And as he leaves say *Rest in peace; your cares are over;*
 *Let the earth lie light upon your bones.*
My warning is true, but truth will not profit me;
 Love has to be pursued on its own terms.
Go on, then, and tell me to sell my forefather's home –
 So be it! – Under the hammer, household gods!
All Circe's, all Medea's poisons,
 All the grasses Thessaly produces,
All the hippomane that drips from mares in heat
 When Venus inspires the invincible herds with passion,
All this mixed with a thousand other herbs I'll drink for her,
 If only my Nemesis will look on me with a kindly eye.

## II.v

Apollo, smile; a new priest steps within your temple;
   Rise up and draw near with your lyre and psalms.
Now stir the speaking strings with your thumb, I beg you;
   Now mould words to the praises I sing.
Visit us, forehead bound with the laurel of triumph;
   Come, while they pile the hearths, to your rites.
Come glistening and beautiful; now put on the vesture
   Laid in store; now comb your long locks well;
Be as they say you were when king Saturn was routed,
   When to victorious Jupiter you chanted paeans of praise.

You see the distant events to come; the augur in your service
   Knows well what fate the prescient birdsong tells.
You govern the fall of lots and the seer's sense of the future,
   When the god marks the slippery entrails with his signs.
Under your guidance the Sibyl never deceived the Romans,
   Chanting their fate hidden in hexameters.
Apollo, let Messalinus touch the consecrated pages
   As your prophet, and visit him and teach him what to declare.
The Sibyl gave oracles to Aeneas, after he had borne off on his
      shoulders
   His father and the Lares he snatched from their shrine,
Believing not in any Rome to be, as from the deep he looked back
      sadly
   At Ilium and his gods, glowing with fire.

(At that time Romulus had not yet shaped the eternal city's
   Walls – uninhabitable as long as Remus had a share –

The grassy Palatine was cropped by heifers
  And humble huts stood on Jove's citadel.
Pan was there splashed with milk in the shade of a holm-oak,
  And Pales, made out of wood with a countryman's knife;
The migrant shepherd's offering hung on a tree-trunk,
  A chattering pipe set aside for the god of the woods –
The kind of pipe with a row of reeds in decreasing order,
  Each stalk joined to its smaller neighbour with wax.
And where the Velabrum now lies exposed could be seen proceeding
  A small boat, driven across the shallows with the stroke of oars.
There on a feast day, soon to find favour with the herd's rich owner,
  A young girl was rowed across to her man;
And with her returned the gifts of a fruitful landscape,
  Cheese, and the white lamb of a snow-white ewe.)


'Unslothful Aeneas, brother of hovering Cupid,
  Carrying your Trojan relics on banished ships,
Jupiter now allots you the fields of Laurentum;
  A hospitable land invites your wandering Lares home.
There you will be worshipped when the venerable stream of Numicus
  Sends you to heaven as the hero-god of the land.
See, Victory hovers above your weary vessels;
  That proud goddess comes at last to the men of Troy.
See, in my eyes fires gleam from the camp of the Rutulians;
  For you, barbarous Turnus, I foretell your death.
I look on the Laurentine camp and the wall of Lavinium
  And Alba Longa built under Ascanius' leadership;
And you too, soon to find favour with Mars, his priestess,
  Ilia, deserter of Vesta's hearth,

And your furtive union and your cast-off chaplet
    And the weapons of the eager god abandoned on the bank.
Crop now, bulls, the grass from the seven hillsides,
    While you can; a great city will be sited here.
Rome! – your name the destiny of the lands you must govern,
    Wherever Ceres looks down on her fields from the sky,
Wherever the gates of the sun's risings open, and in the flowing
        waters
    Wherever the ocean-stream bathes those panting steeds.
Troy indeed will be surprised at itself, confessing
    You looked well to her future on this long road.
I prophesy the truth; as I hope to feed always uninjured
    On the sacred bays, in permanent virginity.'

So chanted the prophetess, and called you to her, Apollo,
    And tossed her streaming hair around her face.
All that Amalthea said, all that Herophile of Marpessus,
    And all the warnings of Phyto of Greece,
And all the fortunes the Sibyl of Tibur carried
    And preserved dry in her bosom through Anio's streams –
These all said that there would be omens of warfare, a comet,
    And told how stones in showers would rain down on the
        earth;
There are stories of trumpets and of arms that were heard
        clashing
    In the sky, and of sacred woods prophesying flight;
The sun itself failed of its light, and the year, cloud-shrouded,
    Saw him yoke horses that had turned pale;
Warm tears are said to have been shed by the gods' statues,
    And bullocks to have found voice and foretold men's fate.

But these things were long ago; be kind now, Apollo,
    And drown these prodigies in the untamed seas;

Let the lighted laurel crack with flames that are holy,
  And with this omen let the year be fortunate and blessed.
When the laurel has given its good omens, be glad, you farmers;
  Ceres will stretch your granaries full with grain;
And, smeared with must, the countryman will pound the clusters,
  Until the great vats and pipkins overflow.
Soaked in the wine the shepherd will celebrate the festival of
      Pales
  In singing; far be you then, you wolves, from the folds.
Deep-drunk he will religiously light the straw-stacks
  And bound across the ritual flames.
The mother will bear children, and the children snatch kisses
  From their parents, grasping them by the ears;
The grandfather will not tire of sitting with his small grandson
  And talking children's prattle, old man with boy.
Then the young people will lie on the grass in the god's service,
  Where the shade of an ancient tree falls light,
And make themselves canopies of their clothes tied up with
      garlands,
  While the cup itself stands crowned with a wreath.
They all shall get a feast for themselves and pile up festival
      tables
  Of turves, and heap up couches too of turves.
Here the drunk youth will load his girl with curses,
  Which later he will wish in his prayers may pass unheard;
Fierce now with his darling, he'll weep when sober
  And swear he must have been deranged.


With your good will, Apollo, let us have an end of bows and
      arrows!
  Simply so that Cupid may walk on earth unarmed.
The skill is laudable; but after Cupid took up shooting,
  How much distress must that skill answer for!

Not least to me, for a year now lying prostrate with my wounds,
   (Since the pain itself brings pleasure, I commend the disease!)
And writing of Nemesis, without whom none of my verses
   Can find just diction, or even properly scan.
For your part, woman, I warn you, spare the god's prophet,
   For their protection keeps the poets safe,
That I may sing Messalinus' praises, as before his chariot
   He carries conquered towns, the reward of war,
Himself wearing the bays; and wreathed with wild bay the soldiers
   Shall loudly chant the old triumphal cry.
Then my adored Messalla shall make for the crowd an exhibition
   Of fatherly love, and as the chariot passes by, applaud.

Be gracious, Apollo; so may your locks remain untonsured:
   So may your sister remain in perennial chastity.

## II.vi

Macer goes off to the army; what will gentle Cupid do?
  Accompany him, and unflinchingly carry weapons round his
      neck?
And will he consent to go armed by his side
  Over long land-routes or the shifting seas?
Burn him, I beg you, boy – the wild one who has left your
      placid occupations,
  And call back the deserter to your flag.
But if you're to spare soldiers, then here's another future soldier
  All set to fetch himself a helmetful of buoyant water.
I'm off to the army – good-bye Venus and good-bye girls;
  I too have strength; I too am glad to hear the trumpet.
I speak grand words – but when I've grandly done so,
  A closed door immediately dashes my brave remarks.
How often have I sworn never to come back to this door-
      step.
  But whenever I swear, though I swear my best, my foot itself
      returns.
Fierce Cupid, if only I might see those weapons of yours, those
      arrows
  Broken, and see your firebrands snuffed!
You rack the wretched; you force me to curse myself
  And speak blasphemies in my distraction.
I would already have ended my hell in death, but that credulous
      hope
  Cherishes life's spark, and always says tomorrow will be better.
Hope feeds farmers, hope lends seed on credit
  To ploughed furrows, to be repaid at heavy interest.

Hope angles for birds with nooses and for fish with rods,
    While the bait conceals till the moment the thin hook.
Hope even consoles a man chained in doughty fetters:
    His legs may clank with iron, and yet he sings as he works.
Hope vows me a compliant Nemesis – and Nemesis says no!
    Please, please don't overwhelm this goddess, cruel girl.
Mercy, I beg you, by the untimely gathered bones of your
        sister:
    So may the little girl rest well beneath a tender earth.
She is one of my special devotions; gifts I will bring
    To her tomb and wreaths wet with my tears.
To her mound I will run and sit in supplication,
    And bemoan my fate in company with her dumb ash.
She will not let her votary on your account be always weep-
        ing;
    As if in words of hers, I forbid you to be so stubborn,
Lest her shade, being of no account with you, may send you
        nightmares,
    And as you doze your sister stand mourning by your bed;
Just as she was when she fell down from the high window,
    And came all bloodied to the lakes below.
I'll stop, lest my mistress' bitter grief should be reawakened:
    I'm not worth so much that she should shed a single tear;
She doesn't deserve to spoil her speaking eyes with weeping;
    Her bawd is the one that hurts me; the girl is good.
Poor me, her go-between Phryne is killing me; how she comes
        and goes
    Carrying tablets hidden away in her bosom.
When I recognize my mistress' sweet tones from the door-
        step,
    She will deny she's even at home.
When a night has been promised me she says the girl is sick
    Or has been panicked by some menace.

Then do I die of anxiety, and my abandoned mind conceives to
itself
  The man who must be holding the girl who is mine, and all the
  different ways of it.
Then, bawd, I summon curses on your head; your life may well
  be full of fears,
  If even the tiniest part of what I say has stirred the gods to
  action.

# BOOK THREE
# THE TIBULLAN
# COLLECTION

## LYGDAMUS

## III.i

The festal first of Roman Mars' month has come –
  The year's rising for our ancestors,
And in regimented progress from all directions run
  Through the city streets and houses presents.
Tell us, Pierides, with what present shall Neaera be honoured,
  My own,
        or still my dear Neaera, even if I am deceived.
*Beautiful girls are caught by rhyme, and greedy ones by profit;*
  *Let her find fitting pleasure, then, in some new verse.*
*But a yellow parchment wrap must shroud the snowy book,*
  *And pumice first shave off the white papyrus whiskers,*
*And the top end of the thin sheet must be fronted*
  *By a label written to mark it with your name;*
*And between the twin finials the rollers must be painted.*
  *In such neat trim, and only such, must the work be sent.*
You –
  inspiration of this poem of mine –
                I beg you
  By the Castalian cool and the Pierian basins,
Go to the house, and give her this,
                my well-groomed book,
  Just as it is;
  let none of its fresh hue fade.
She'll respond, if my love for her is shared,
  Or if it's less –
                even if I've fallen from her heart.

But first present her, as she merits, with expansive salutations,
   And then in humble tones address these words:
*Your former husband, now your brother, honourable Neaera,*
   *Sends these words, and asks you to accept this little gift.*
*He swears you're more dear to him than the marrow of his bones,*
   *Either as his wife or as his future sister;*
*Preferably his wife; hope of this title shall only be*
   *Removed from him in death by Dis' pale water.*

III.ii

He was iron –

the first who stole a boy's darling from him,
    And darling boy from girl;
And he was hard too, who could bear such pain –
    Had power to live –

his mate torn from his side.
In this I am not firm

my qualities do not include such im-
passiveness:
    Pain cracks stout hearts.
Nor do I blush to speak truth

and of my life confess weariness has
come to birth,
    After such long suffering.
So, when I am changed into insubstantial shadow,
    When white bones are hid with mantle of black ash,
Before my pyre

long locks dishevelled
    Let Neaera come

and let her mourn and weep –
Come, partnered by the grief of her dear mother –
    She to her son-in-law

she mourning to her man;
Address my spirit, and my fresh ghost,
    Then bathe their loyal hands in water;
And after this – the sole part of my body that survives,
my bones,
    In ungirdled black pick out gleaming.

And having gathered them, first wet them with old wine,
   Then go to plunge them also in white milk,
Then take the moisture off in linen towels,
   And lay them dry in their new marble home.
There what merchandise wealthy Panchaia sends
   The eastern Arabs and rich Assyria
Be poured,
                      tears too that remember me;
   So would I wish to be laid when turned to but bone.
But let a title demonstrate my death's unhappy cause,
   And on the tomb's face where people pass
                  these lines make me known:
*Lygdamus here is laid; long pain and concern for Neaera –*
   *Wife that was torn from his side – caused him to sicken and die.*

## III.iii

I've filled the sky with promises, Neaera,
    And offered appeasing incense with my many prayers
                but to what advantage?
Not that I might step from the doorway of a marble palace
    Marked out and conspicuous for my glorious house;
Or that bulls of mine might renew wide acres
    And the kindly earth give up great harvests;
But to share the joys of a long lifetime with you,
    And that my declining years might fall to rest in your bosom,
At the time when I have filled full my measured span of daylight
    And must go naked on the ferry of Lethe.
I've no use
                for the heavy weight of wealthy gold
    Nor if my fertile ploughland were cleft by a thousand oxen,
  Nor for a house propped up on Phrygian pillars
    (Yours, perhaps, Taenarus, or yours, Carystus),
  Nor forests in my courts mimicking the sacred groves,
    Nor gilded beams and marble floors;
No pleasure in the pearl that's picked on the Red Sea shore,
    Nor the wool dyed with the purple-fish of Sidon,
  Nor whatever else the world admires.
                In them lies envy.
    Most things the people love they love misguidedly.
Men's minds and cares are not relieved by wealth,
    For Fortune rules our days by her own laws.
Let me have happy poverty with you, Neaera;
    Without you I have no wish for kings' gifts –
                none of them.

O snow-white dawn that will restore you to me!
   O thrice and four times happy day!
But if, whatever I promise for your sweet return,
   My god turns his ear away and will not listen,
Then kingdoms have no pleasure for me
                              nor the golden river of Lydia
   Nor all the wealth the world's circumference holds.
Others may long for it;
                              but I would enjoy a poor man's
                                                    lifestyle
   Free from care – with my dear wife.
Be present, Saturn's daughter, forward my timid prayers;
   Forward them, you of Cyprus, riding on your scallop.
If Fate and the ill-omened sisters refuse her return –
   Those who draw the threads and prophesy the future –
Let pale Orcus,
                              the wealthy one, in his sluggish
                                                    streams,
   Call me to his vast-spread rivers and his dusky swamp.

## III.iv

The gods bring better things; let the dreams not be true
    That a terrible sleep brought me last night.
Go far away, you vanities; turn your false appearances else-
        where;
    Do not try to find credence in me any more.
The gods give true monition; heralds of future fate,
    The entrails scrutinized by men of Etruria
                give true monition:
But what of dreams? Do they delude us in the cheating night
             – at random?
    And make the panic-stricken mind fear nothings?
And is the terror empty that makes men propitiate the omens of
        the night
    With religiously sprinkled flour and dancing grains of
        salt?
And yet however things are –
                whether men are given true monition,
    Or put trust in dreams that lie –
I pray to Lucina to make my night-fears groundless,
    And to will it that I shall have been causelessly terrified –
              having deserved no such thing,
Provided that my heart is subject to the guilt of no foul deed,
    And that my tongue has not blasphemed against the mighty
        gods.


Now Night behind black mares had paced out the upper firma-
        ment
    And sluiced his wheels in the opaque blue stream;

The god that profits sick hearts had not yet drugged me;
    Sleep falters before reaching my troubled house.
At last, when Phoebus gazed out over his rising rim,
    A late repose dragged down my weary eyelids.
Then I dreamed that a youthful figure –
                forehead bound with innocent bay –
    Set foot in my apartment.
No other age of former men saw anything more beautiful;
    No house of human beings could today.
His undocked hair rippled round his long neck;
    On his myrrh-splashed locks stood beads of Syrian dew.
He gleamed and dazzled like Leto's daughter Luna –
    On his white body a pink suffusion,
Like the flush on the tender cheek of a virgin,
    As her face glows when they lead her first to her youthful
        husband,
Or like white lilies which girls interweave with amaranth,
    Or pale fruits reddening in the autumn.
I saw dancing on his heels the hem of his tragedian's robe –
    Such was the clothing that his gleaming body wore.
A work, of rare skill, shining with tortoiseshell and ivory,
    His speaking lyre, hung by his left side.
As he first approached he played the notes with an ivory quill,
    And sang songs to cheer the heart from his resonant lips;
His fingers and his voice spoke together then,
    But soon in sweet monody he voiced these gloomy words:
'Hail, favourite of the gods: for to a god-fearing poet
    Phoebus, Bacchus and the Muses show due favour;
Yet Semele's child Bacchus and the inventive sisters
    Do not know the art of telling what tomorrow's hour will
        bring,
Whereas to me the Father gave the power of seeing destiny's laws,
    And things that will come to pass in future years.

Listen then to what I say, a prophet whose words will not prove
    false,
      And understand why the mouth of the god of Cynthus is
      reputed true.
She who is as dear to you
                      as no daughter to her mother,
      As no attractive girl to her eager lover;
   For whom you besiege the powers above with prayers;
      Who will let pass none of your days untroubled,
   And when sleep has shrouded you in his dusky cloak
      Idly teases you with nocturnal picturings;
She, made famous in your poetry, the beautiful Neaera,
      Prefers to be another lover's mistress.
Her heart knows no bond; she flings her attachment in all
      quarters –
      And Neaera is not pleased with marriage in an unadul-
      terated home.
O cruel sex! O fickle name of woman!
      Accursed be any woman who has learned to mock a hus-
      band!
And yet she can be swayed; women's minds are malleable;
      Only reach out your hands and entreat her hard.
Love in his cruelty has schooled us to attempt mighty labours;
      In his cruelty Love has taught us to bear beatings.
The story that I Apollo once fed Admetus' snow-white cows
      Was not invented to beget idle laughter.
At that time I could take no pleasure in my resonant lyre,
      Or mould my voice to match its strings;
But I practised ditties on a pierced oatstraw,
  I – the son of Jupiter and Leto.
Young man, you do not know the nature of love, if you refuse to
      tolerate
      A savage mistress and a ruthless marriage.

So do not delay in bringing to bear your winning cries of woe;
    Hard hearts are overborne by melting prayers.
But if the oracles in my sacred temples prophesy the truth,
    In my name take back to her this message:
*"This marriage bed the Delian god assures you:*
    *In this you are happy; cease to want another lover."'*


He spoke; and idle sleep melted from my body.
    Ah, grant I may never see such misery!
I could not have believed your longings so at odds with mine,
    Or that your heart could contain such shortcomings.
For the vast wide sea was not your parent,
    Nor Chimaera, rolling fireballs from her savage jaws,
Nor the dog maned with a squadron of snakes,
    With three tongues and triple head,
Nor Scylla's virgin body sheathed with dogs;
    No savage lioness conceived and bore you,
Nor the barbarous land of Scythia, or the terrible Syrtis –
    But a humane home, with no place for the ruthless,
And a mother far gentler than all other women,
    And a father equal to anyone for his friendliness.


Such was my cruel dream, and may the god make good of it;
    And tell the warm south wind to carry it away into the void.

## III.v

You on the one hand are detained
>                    where the water drips from Etruscan
>                                                    springs
>   (*Do not go near that pool around the dog-time of summer*)
>   So nearly equal to the god's waters at Baiae,
>     Now when the ground bursts out in springtime pink:
Look at me on the other hand –
>     to me Persephone announces the black hour –
>     Don't hurt me, goddess, who have done nothing to deserve
>       it.
I haven't outraged the rites forbidden to men,
>                    the rites of the Praise-worthy God-
>                                                    dess, nor told of them;
>     I have not made so bold.
My hand has not adulterated someone's cup with essences to
>       strike him dead,
>     Or administered a dose of pounded poison;
Or done sacrilege, pressing a lighted brand against a temple wall.
>     There are no crimes against nature gnawing my conscience.
I have not wildly muttered pent-up insults
>     Or opened a blasphemous mouth against the gods.
Nor have the white hairs yet despoiled the black,
>     Nor has bent-backed and loitering senility arrived.
My year of birth, when first my parents saw me,
>     Was the year coincident Fate felled both consuls together.
It brings no satisfaction to cheat the vine just when the grapes
>       begin to swell,
>     Or tug down apples only that minute come to being.

You, in charge of the ghostly rivers, don't touch me,
    You gods that drew the third lot, the merciless kingdom.
One day I want to be allowed to see and know the Elysian fields,
    The hulk that floats on Lethe and the Cimmerian lakes;
But only when I see my old face sallow and wrinkled
    And find myself telling the young about the good old days.
If only I were now terrified by a fever without substance –
    But for fifteen days my limbs have been weak and limp.
Meanwhile, you there in Etruria,
    you pay your regular attentions to the divinities of the water;
    The easy yielding water swirls from slow-swinging arms.
Live the good life, but don't forget me as you do so –
    Still alive, maybe; or maybe fate has now wished me gone.
Meanwhile promise Dis some black animals
    And a libation of wine and white milk.

## III.vi

Be at my side, shining Bacchus; and I will pray
                    you may keep always the vine of your
                                        mysteries,
   And always wear the ivy twined around your brows.
Yourself remove my pain: your cup be my doctor;
   'Whelmed by that gift, love has fallen before now.
Dear boy, soak the cups in the ancestral vintage,
   Pour us the Falernian till your hand is horizontal.
Go far away, you ruthless creature, care, go far, tribulations;
   Shed your radiance here, Delian god, with your snow-
      white birds.
You, sweet friends, consent to my considered purpose;
   Under my flag let none of you withold your company;
And if one does refuse a mild drinking engagement,
   Let his girl be unfaithful and never be found out.
That god makes bold spirits mild, bruises the fierce,
   And sends him in submission to his mistress' assize,
Bows Armenian tigers and tawny lionesses,
   And gives the indomitable sensitive hearts.
Love too can do all this and more. But ask this gift of Bacchus:
   Which of you will benefit from cups of sobriety?
Bacchus comes on equal terms and not at all terrible to those
   Who pay respect to him and to the laughter-making vine;
But he comes in anger, anger and more than anger, to the strict:
   If you fear the great power of an angry god, then drink.
The type and severity of penalty that he threatens
   We can learn from the bloody plunder of that Theban
      mother.

But from this company such fears may be far removed – it is
      Neaera, if anyone,
  I pray to feel the force of the injured god's rage.
What a request, fool! Winds, carry away my rash prayer,
  And with the airy clouds make it your plunder.
Although there is no concern left in you for me, Neaera,
  Be prosperous, and your star shine bright.
As for us, we must devote these moments to the carefree table;
  After so many, one cloudless day has come at last.
But ah, how hard it is to pretend a joy one does not feel,
  How hard to mould a gloomy mind to making merry.
A hypocritical mouth is not the best for constructing smiles,
  And drunken words sound wrong in careworn men.
But what are these complaints? You ugly preoccupations, remove
      yourselves;
  The father we call Lenaeus hates such pessimism.
O Cretan girl, you the forswearing of Theseus' tongue,
  You wept alone – abandoned – to an unfamiliar sea:
Thus, daughter of Minos, the wise Catullus wrote on your
      behalf,
  Recalling the irreligious deed of an ungrateful man.
But now I warn you others too: happy the man who from
      another's pain
  Can learn to beware his own –
Not to let arms that hang around your neck deceive you,
  Or a mercenary tongue with its ingratiating prayers;
Though she has sworn (but to deceive you) by her own dear
      eyes,
  By her Juno, by Venus, the divinities of women,
There will be no truth in her oaths:

                  Jupiter laughs at the perjuries of
                              lovers,
  And tells the winds to sweep them away as of no account.

So why? Why do I complain of the words of a girl so many times
    a liar?
    Let me have no more business with serious talk!
How much I could wish to rest long nights with you
    And in your company wake long days,
You, so unfaithful, and unfaithful not in tune with my deserts,
    And yet, however unfaithful, still beloved.
But Bacchus loves the nymph of water: why so slow, you sluggard
    steward?
    Bring the best Marcian water to dilute this ancient wine.
For my part, if a frivolous girl avoids the company of my table
    Out of desire for a bed not yet familiar,
Am I to reiterate my sighs the whole night long?
    Come boy, pour in the stream of wine a little more resolutely;
I ought to have drenched my temples with Syrian nard a long
    time back,
    And twined my hair with garlands.

III.vii    PANEGYRIC OF MESSALLA

Of you, Messalla, will I sing, although
Your virtue once disclosed does but dismay:
Although my weak strength cannot stand upright,
Yet I'll begin, and if my song falls short
Of your just praise, and I'm too poor a soul
To couch such deeds, and no one but yourself
Could weave your actions on the pages' loom
So that they were not greater than the words,
It will be satisfaction to have tried.
Do not reject my little offering;
Even Phoebus found the gifts the Cretan brought
Very acceptable; and Icarus
Gave more delight to Bacchus as a host
Than anyone – as testify the stars
On clear nights, Sirius and Erigone,
That no succeeding age deny the tale.
Indeed Alcides, destined as a god
To climb Olympus, gladly laid his feet
Beneath Molorchus' roof; handfuls of flour
Have pacified celestial gods ere now,
And other beasts have fallen on their hearths
Than bulls with gilded horns. Let this please too,
This tiny effort, that in gratitude
I may compose more verses and yet more.
    Let others tell the great world's wonderful
Construction, and what kind of land it was
That sank down in the unmeasured void of space,
What sea that in curved orbit washed it round,

* Brackets indicate original Latin line numbers.

The wayward air and how it tries to rise
From earth, and fiery ether flowing round
Connected to it, and how all things finally
Are closed in by the overhanging sky:
But all to which my native muse aspires,
Whether it's equal, or, which hope denies,
Surpasses you, or falls short (certainly
My muse will fall short), all I dedicate
To you; let not my page want your great name,
For though the praises of your ancient race
O'erflow your cup, your pride is not content
With your ancestors' fame; you do not ask
What ev'ry portrait's legend has to tell –
You strive to excel the honours of the past,
Shedding more lustre on posterity
Than your proud ancestors could shed on you.
Your portrait's label will not hold your deeds,
You'll have great volumes of undying verse,
Men will convene, greedy to write your praise
In poetry and prose, from ev'ry side;
They will compete to be preferred by you:
May I be the successful one, to inscribe
My name above the tale of those great acts.

For who in camp or forum has done deeds
Greater than yours? Not that in either sphere
The praise is less or more; as just scales hang
With level beam, and when unequal loads
Depress the pans, the beam floats out of true,
Yet sinks no more on this side than on that
It rises, as its courses alternate.

If the perverse crowd's fickle passions buzz,
No other can calm them so well as you.
Or if a judge's animosity

Must be assuaged, your words can make him mild.
Pylos and Ithaca are not supposed
To have begotten such great men, in Nestor
And Ulysses – his small state's glorious crown –
Though one lived to be old, while Titan ran
Three fertile generations through, and th' other
Roamed boldly through cities unknown to man,
Where land is closed in by the outer waves.
He trounced the bands of Cicones in war;
The lotus could not turn aside his course;
Etna's inhabitant, great Neptune's son,
Submitted, overcome by Maron's wine,
His eyesight ravished; Ulysses sailed on
Across mild seas, Aeolus' winds his freight,
And so drew near the brute Laestrygones
And king Antiphates, a land well watered
By the cold stream of famed Artacie.
He alone changed not with wise Circe's cup,
Although the sun begot her, skilled to alter
Either with herbs or spells men's former shapes.
He even reached the dark Cimmerian walls,
On whom day never shone from the bright East,
Whether the sun drove high or under earth.
He saw the gods' great offspring, how they gave
Law to the light shades bound to Pluto's realm;
And with swift bark passed by the Sirens' shore.
Nor, as he floated on twin deaths' confines,
Could Scylla's cruel-mawed onset frighten him
Savagely snaking through the snapping waves,
And wild Charybdis could not suck him down
Either by towering up sheer from her bed
Or stripping bare the sea's arrested flow.
And let me not pass over in my tale

The wandering sun-god's ravished feeding-stock,
Calypso's love and fertile fields, and last,
Phaeacia and his wretched wanderings' end.
Whether these woes were felt in Roman lands,
Or if story has opened up new worlds
To place his journeys in, he bears the palm
For hardihood – you for your eloquence.

   No other man's mind has a tighter hold
On the arts of war, where it is fit to draw
A safe ditch round a camp, how best to fix
Barbed stakes against the foe, what ground is best
To enclose with ramparts, where the earth projects
The sweet spring water, how to make the approach
Easy for your side, but hard for the foe,
How the men thrive on rivalry for praise,
Who throws the slow shaft best, who best can shoot
The speedy arrow, who with the tough spear
Can best break through all obstacles, and who
Can check the swift horse with a tightened bit
And give the sluggish one the slackened rein,
By turns in straight line hasten on, or else
With curved gyration swing sharp round,
Who wants to guard himself with small round shield,
Who with his right hand and who with his left,
As from each side the foeman's onset comes,
Or reach the set target with whirling sling;
Let bold Mars' contests come, and lines prepare
With hostile flags to charge at one another,
Then you'll not fail to set your face to fight,
If the array must form into a square,
So that the line may charge with balanced brows,
Or if you wish on two fronts separately
To clear the issue, so those on the right

Hold up the left, the left supports the right,
And thus you win a double victory.
My lines of praise do not proceed through doubts:
I sing of things proved by the test of war.
The brave troops of conquered Iapydia
Bear witness, and the false Pannonian,
Scattered pell-mell across the ice-bound Alps,
And that poor man born at Arupium –
If once you saw his head unbowed by age,
You would be less amazed at Pylos' fame,
And Nestor's span of three whole generations;
For while the old man passes his long life,
Titan will have renewed a hundred years;
Yet he himself entrusts his nimble frame
To a speeding horse, and with strong rein sits there
Controlling it: faced by your generalship,
But never else, Domator turned his back
And bowed his free neck to the Roman chain.

   Nor will you be content with all of this;
Greater things press behind what is achieved,
As I have learned from omens that speak truth,
Such as not even Melampus could outdo.
You had just donned a robe that blazed with purple,
As the day dawned that ushers in the year,
When the sun raised its head from the clear waves
In greater splendour, and the waning winds
Held back their wild blasts, while the winding streams
No more pursued their former paths. Indeed
The whirling sea stood still, its breakers calmed,
No bird slid through the breezes of the sky,
And no rough animal cropped the thick woods
But it gave generous silence for your prayers;
Jupiter drove his light car through the void

To stand by you, leaving sky-capped Olympus,
And with attentive ear applied himself
To listen to your prayers; to all of them
He nodded his unfailing head; the fire
Lapt up brighter above the altar-piles.

  So, with gods' encouragement, press on
To greater things; let not your triumph be
Like other men's. Gaul shall not hold you back,
With nearby wars, though it lies in your path,
Nor bold Spain's broad domains, nor that fierce land
Settled by colonists from Thera's isle,
Nor that washed by the Nile, or kingly streams
Of royal Choaspes, or the rapid Gyndes
That maddened Cyrus, or the Oroatis,
Nor yet the land where Tamyris marked off
Her realm at the Araxes' winding course,
Or the Padaean, Phoebus' neighbour, holds
His distant fields and celebrates his feast
At tables spread with cannibal repast,
Or where the Hebrus and the Tanais
Water the Getae and the Magyni.
But why stop here? Wherever ocean's stream
Bounds in the world, no region will oppose
Itself to you in arms. Britain awaits you,
Unconquered yet by Roman arms; so too
The world's opposite quarter, which the sun
Divides by his whole course, waits there for you;
For Earth is set surrounded by the air
And overall is ranged into five parts;
Two parts are ravaged by perpetual frost:
There too the land is hid in thick dark shade,
And water never flows right through its course
But freezes hard into thick ice and snow,

Because there Titan never rises high;
The middle part lies always underneath
The heat of Phoebus, whether circling near
The Earth in summer, or in winter days
Hurrying to bring the daylight to an end:
The ground will not rise when the plough bears down,
The crops provide no ears, the fields no grass,
No god, Bacchus, or Ceres, tills the soil,
No animals inhabit this scorched region;
Between it and the frozen quarter lies
A fertile tract, our world, and opposite
To that we know, a second, both of which
The neighbouring climate tempers from both sides,
As the air of each destroys the other's power:
Hence calmly turns our year the seasons' course:
Hence too the bull has learnt to take the yoke,
And the tough vine to climb the highest boughs,
The yearly crop is sheared of its ripe fruits,
Hence iron stirs up the earth and bronze the sea,
And towns indeed rise up with high-built walls.
So, when your feats demand due celebration,
In both spheres you alone will be called great.

My powers are not enough to advertise
Such glory, even though Phoebus himself
Were to dictate my lines; you have at hand
Valgius to gird himself for such a task:
No one is nearer to immortal Homer.
My toil does not span times of languid ease,
Since hostile Fate, as always, wears me down;
Who, when my high house rested on great wealth,
Had ranks of yellow furrows to enrich
My fertile harvests for the time of want;
Whose flocks cropped hillsides in a dense array,

Sufficient for their lord, enough and more
For thief and wolf: I, who had all this wealth,
Now live with want; my troubles are renewed
When long-remembering pain recalls past years.
But even if a harsher fate awaits,
And I am robbed of what is left to me,
My muse will never fail to sing your praise.
Nor will the Muses' due alone be yours;
For you I'd dare to cross the rushing waves,
Though winter's sea were swollen with adverse winds;
For you I'd stand alone before the dense
Squadrons of war, or throw my tiny body
To Etna's flames: whatever I am is yours.
If you have any care, however small,
For me, I would not rather have the realm
Of Lydia, or great Gylippus' fame,
Nor wish to excel the page of Meles' son.
But if my verses, whether all of them,
Or less than all, are either known to you,
Or stray but on the surface of your lips,
The fates shall set no ending to my lays.
Even when the mound is strewn above my bones,
Whether an early day speeds on my death,
Or a long life awaits, whether my shape
Is metamorphosized into a horse
Tutored to scorn the hard plains, or a bull,
The pride of the slow herd, or else a bird
Transported through clear air on feathered wings,
Whenever the long course of passing time
Receives me back as man, I will resume,
And bind new pages to my former books.

## 'GARLAND OF SULPICIA'

### III.viii

For you Sulpicia is dressed, great Mars, on your Kalends;
    Won't you come down in person to gaze at her from heaven?
Venus will pardon you: but, god of violence, be careful
    In case you drop your arms and disgrace yourself as you stare;
When he wants to consume the gods with fire,
    Hot Love lights two firebrands at Sulpicia's eyes.
Whatever she does, wherever her path is directed,
    Grace orders everything unseen and follows on her steps.
If she lets down her hair, then flowing hair will best suit her;
    If she has combed it up, she must be adored for her coiffure.
She inflames desire if she chooses to walk out in a Tyrian cloak,
    And no less so if she comes to you in a robe of snow –
Just as the god of good omen Vertumnus in eternal Olympus
    Has a thousand guises, and wears each one so that it suits him.
Alone of young women she is worthy to be given by Tyre
    Soft fleeces twice soaked in her costly dyes,
And to possess all that in his sweet-smelling fields is harvested
    By the rich Arab that cultivates his crop of scents,
And whatever gems are gathered from the Red Sea shore by the
        black Indian,
    The neighbour of the waters of the dawn.

Sing of her on these festal Kalends, Pierian choir,
    And you, Phoebus, proud in your tortoise lyre.
This ceremonial rite shall she receive for many a year;
    No woman is worthier of your dancing band than her.

## III.ix

Spare my young man, boar, on the good pastures of the
      plain,
  Or frequenting the by-ways of the shadowy mountain.
Don't take it upon you to whet your merciless tusks for the
      battle,
  And allow his guardian, Love, to keep him safe for me.
But the goddess of Delos draws him away with his concern for
      hunting:
  Confound all forests and let the race of dogs become ex-
      tinct!
What craze is this, what mad disposition to hem thick woods with
      a circle,
  And so willingly allow those tender hands to be hurt?
What good is it stealthily to enter the lairs of wild animals
  And mark those ivory legs on barbed brambles?
And yet, Cerinthus, if I could roam in your company,
  I myself would carry the plaited nets across the hills.
I'd search myself for the tracks of the fast-running deer,
  And remove the iron collar from the speeding dog.
Only then, my darling, would I take pleasure in a forest,
  If it were proved I had lain down with you there by the
      traps;
And then, although he comes to the nets, the boar will be off
      untouched –
  He could not be allowed to disturb the joys of greedy Love.
Without my presence there must be no love – you must touch
      those nets, my boy,
  With unentangled hands, in utter chastity;

And I pray that any girl who snakes in furtively to the place of
     my love
  Falls for their plunder to the beasts of prey.
You must leave this enthusiasm for the hunt to your father,
  And yourself run quickly back to my arms.

## III.x

Approach and expel the tender young girl's illness,
　　Approach, Apollo, proud in your uncropped hair.
Believe me, you must be quick; after this, Apollo, never will you
　　　　regret
　　Laying your healing hands on beauty.
See that no wasting sickness usurps her pale members,
　　And no ugly blotches mark her fainting limbs.
Whatever is bad, whatever sets the weight of fear upon our
　　　　hearts,
　　Let rivers with their rushing waters carry to the ocean.
Come, holy one, bring with you all the fragrances
　　And all the incantations that relieve tired bodies.
End the young man's torture – he fears his girl is doomed,
　　And for his mistress' life he makes innumerable promises.
Sometimes he prays, and now, when she seems to weaken,
　　He voices harsh words against the immortal gods.
But shed your fear, Cerinthus; the god does not harm lovers.
　　Only keep true to your love and your girl is safe.
No need for crying; it will be a fitter time for tears
　　If ever she gets out of sorts with you.
Now she is totally your own; with shining face she only dreams
　　　　of you;
　　Ill-founded the hopes in which the young men sit round
　　　　her.
Apollo, be gracious; great will be your tribute of glory,
　　If in one healed body you resuscitate two lives.

Happy then, and fitly honoured you will be, when both of them
    in gratitude
  Compete to accomplish on your consecrated altar what they
    vowed.
Then the respectful throng of gods will all congratulate you;
  Each one will wish that he himself possessed your skills.

## III.xi

Today, the day that gave you to me, Cerinthus,
  Shall be a dedicated day and always counted among the feasts.
At your birth the fates declared a new régime of slavery for
      women,
  And gave you the proud monarchy over them.
But I am more on fire than any other. It pleases me, Cerinthus,
      to be so,
  If in your heart there is a corresponding flame for me.
Let our love be shared, I ask you by those sweet sweet robberies,
  By your very eyes, and your guardian-spirit.
Good spirit, be pleased to take my incense and approve my prayer,
  If only, that is, when Cerinthus thinks of me, he too is
      warmed.
But if it happens that at this moment he sighs with love for
      another,
  Then, holy one, I pray you abandon his faithless hearth.
Venus, do not be unjust; either both of us should equally be
      your slaves,
  Or you should lighten my chains.
But rather let both of us be held in a strong chain,
  That no day hereafter is to find the power to loosen.
The young man's wishes are the same as mine, but less openly
      admitted –
  His modesty won't let him say these words out loud.
But you, birthday-spirit, since as a god you are aware of every-
      thing,
  Nod your approval; what difference if his request is secret or
      open?

III.xii

uno, birthday-goddess, receive the dedicated mounds of incense,
　　Which with her tender hand this accomplished girl presents.
Today she is all yours, for you she has dressed herself joy-
　　　　fully,
　　To stand in front of your altar for all to see.
On her part, you are the justification for all these fineries,
　　Though there is someone else she would secretly like to
　　　　please.
But give her your approval, holy goddess, and let no one split the
　　　　lovers,
　　But forge for the youth, I beg you, fetters to match hers.
This is the way to join them well; there's no girl more deserving
　　Of his service, and no man more worthy of her.
The eager pair must not be caught together by any watchful
　　　　guardian;
　　A thousand ways of tricking him must be produced by Cupid's
　　　　art.
Give assent with a sign, and come shimmering in your bright-
　　　　dyed dress.
　　Three offerings are made in meal-cake, three in wine, chaste
　　　　goddess,
And the sedulous mother lectures what to wish for to her
　　　　daughter,
　　While she prays quite otherwise in her unvoiced thought.
Inside her, like the leaping flames that scorch the altar, a fire is
　　　　lit,
　　And even if she could, she would not wish to be unharmed by
　　　　it.

Be gratified by our offerings, Juno, and at the full circle of the
      year,
  Let the love they pray for, now long-established, still be
      theirs.

### SULPICIA

III.xiii

Love at last has come to me, and such, that there'd be more
        immodesty
    In being known to have veiled it from anyone, than to have
        laid it bare;
Thanks to the importunity of my poetry
    Venus has brought him to my breast and laid him there.
She has kept her promise; and anyone whose own bliss
    Shall be said to have passed him by – let him tell mine for
        his.
It is not my will to lay anything in trust to sealed-up wax,
    So none may read me before my lover;
But my erring thrills me, and my features, set wearily for
        Reputation's sake, must needs relax;
    For both of us, soon they'll say, could find none better than
        each other.

## III.xiv

My birthday is near and I hate it, because it must be spent
    On a tedious estate, and (day of ill-omen!) without Cerinthus
        there.
What's nicer than town? Or is a country farm a fit lodgement
    For a girl – a farm in the Arretine plain with its cold river?
Be at ease now, cousin Messalla, you take my part too zealously;
    Roads are not always seasonable for travelling.
Though dragged away, I leave behind my thought and feeling,
    Since force will not let me decide my own life's destiny.

## III.xv

Do you know that your girl is spared that ill-conceived migration?
   She may now be in Rome on her own birthday.
Let us all celebrate that day as a true feast day,
   Which has come your way perhaps beyond your expectation.

## III.xvi

I'm pleased you're so liberal to yourself through confidence in
 me,
 Unafraid that I may foolishly come to grief in female vanity.
Care more for your toga, then, or for some wool-basket-
  burdened whore,
 More than for Sulpicia, daughter of Servius!
But some are worried on my account, who could be pained by
  nothing more,
 Than that for a strange woman's bed I should take second
  place.

## III.xvii

Cerinthus, do you feel for your mistress due concern,
  For the fever in which my weary limbs now toss and turn.
I could not ever wish to master this depressing malady,
  Unless I thought you also wished me to;
What could I gain in mastering it, if you
  Could view my sorry state so unemotionally?

## III.xviii

Never again be so consumed by ardour for me, darling,
 As you were a few nights past, it seemed to me,
If ever I confess to more regret for anything
 I may have done in my youthful stupidity,
Than for the fact that I left you and we spent last night apart
 Through my desire to hide from you the fire in my own heart.

UNKNOWN AUTHOR

III.xix

No woman shall set your bed at a distance from me;
  This was the treaty-stone where our first love was sealed.
You are the only one to satisfy; besides you, in my eyes,
  Not one girl in town could ever be thought beautiful.
If only I could be the only one to think you pretty –
  Displease all others, and I shall be secure.
No need for anyone to envy me; far from me be common boast-
    ing;
  Wise men will feed their joy in the silence of the heart.
In this way I may live happy in some secluded forest,
  Where no path was ever worn by human feet.
You are my repose from care, you, even in blackest night,
  Are light to me, you, in a desolation, are my company.
Although a mistress should be sent Tibullus from on high,
  She will be sent in vain, and love come to no fruition.
This I swear to you by the inviolable divinity of your Juno,
  The goddess whom alone above all others I count great.
But what have I done, poor fool? I have given up my power to
    bargain.
  A mad oath to have sworn! Your fears for me were my advan-
    tage.
Now you'll be brave, now you'll burn me more boldly.
  My wretched chattering tongue has gotten me this ill.
Now, do whatever you like, I will be yours for ever;
  I will not be a runaway from the mistress that I know,
But I will sit bound by the altars of inviolable Venus,
  Who brands the unjust and is gracious to the suppliant.

## III.xx

Your girl is frequently unfaithful, Rumour says;
   Now how I wish I had deaf ears.
Such charges are not made without my great distress.
   Why torture me in my unhappiness, bitter Rumour? – Cease!

# GLOSSARY OF PROPER NAMES

*Cross-references in the glossary are printed in italics.*

ADMETUS: King of Pherae in Thessaly. For love of him *Apollo* bound himself, to serve as his herdsman.

ADOUR: River rising in the Pyrenees and flowing through the territory of the Tarbelli to the Bay of Biscay.

AENEAS: Mythical ancestor of Rome, a Trojan prince who escaped from the Greek sack of Troy, taking with him the hearth-fire and the cult-images of the gods of his house, to found a new city, wherever Destiny should indicate. He was the son of Anchises by the goddess *Venus*, and hence (II.v.39) half-brother to *Cupid*.

AEOLUS: God of the winds, who enclosed the winds in a bag, which he gave to *Ulysses* in order to ensure him a calm voyage. Later they were let out.

AFRICA: (II.iii.62) Carthage in North Africa exported a crimson or scarlet dye of vegetable extraction.

ALBA LONGA, ALBA: The settlement founded by Ascanius, son of *Aeneas*, near the Mons Albanus; the mother city of Rome, situated (I.vii.57) just off the part of the Via Flaminia that *Messalla* repaired for Augustus after the civil wars; called 'gleaming' perhaps simply as a pun on its name ('albus' is the Latin for white), and possibly because of the appearance of the local grey limestone.

ALCIDES: Hercules, reckoned to be the grandson of Alcaeus.

AMALTHEA: A name associated with the *Sibyl* in various places, particularly with the Sibyl of Cumae who sold the original Sibylline books to King Tarquin.

ANIO: Tributary of the Tiber, which flows through Tibur (modern Tivoli), where there are beautiful falls and cataracts.

ANTIPHATES: King of the *Laestrygones*.

APOLLO: Greek god adopted by Rome very early in her history; associated with prophecy, archery, and healing; also with the sun, just as his sister *Diana* was with the moon; also patron of the musical and literary arts and leader of the *Muses*; he and Diana were the

*Glossary*

twin children of Jupiter by *Leto*, born at *Delos*; known by several
other names, particularly *Phoebus*, and names derived from his
principal shrines, such as *Delphi* and *Cynthus*; in art and sculpture
always youthful and long haired. (II.iii.11) Lover of *Admetus*.

AQUITANIA: The part of southern France bounded by the river
Garonne, the Bay of Biscay, and the Pyrenees. *Messalla*'s victories
there earned him a triumph.

ARAB: Arabia was one of the several areas loosely conceived as the
home of perfumes and spices, and other luxuries (cf. *Armenia* and
*Assyria*).

ARAXES: River of Armenia, flowing east to the Caspian Sea.

ARMENIA: Thought to be the source of spices and perfumes, many of
which merely came through Armenia from further east and south-
east; also the home of lions and tigers.

ARRETINE field and its cold river (III.xiv.4). Arretium is the modern
Arezzo in Tuscany, and its river is the Arno which rises in the
Apennines nearby.

ARTACIE: A spring in the land of the *Laestrygones*.

ARUPIUM: Town in the territory of the *Iapydians* in the north-
west of present-day Yugoslavia.

ASCANIUS: Son of *Aeneas* and founder of *Alba Longa*.

ASSYRIA: One of the lands at the far end of the eastern caravan route
which brought so many luxuries to the Roman world.

AUDE: A river rising in the Pyrenees and flowing to the Mediterranean
near Narbonne.

AUSTER: The south-west wind, which commonly brought rainy
weather.

BACCHUS: Originally an Italian vegetation-spirit; became identified
with the Greek Dionysus; hence he is primarily the god of the
vine and its products, but also the centre of a frenzied orgiastic
cult – his title Lenaeus (III.vi.38) was connected with this cult; son
of *Semele* by Zeus, and father of *Priapus*; like *Apollo*, represented
in art as possessed of eternal youth and flowing hair; for the story
of Bacchus and Icarus (III.vii.9), see under *Icarus*.

BAIAE: A favourite coastal resort; its hot springs were, as always,
sacred to Hercules.

157

BELLONA: I.vi.45ff. – not here the old Italian goddess of war, but an import from Cappadocia. Her worship was conducted as described here, by Cappadocian priests.

BIRTHDAY-SPIRIT: See *Natalis*.

BONA DEA: A mystery-cult famous for its exclusion of males – the sight of the ritual was supposed to turn male eyes blind (cf. III.v.7).

CALYPSO: A nymph who detained *Ulysses* on her island for eight years, promising him immortality in return for marriage. Finally she gave him the tools to build a raft.

CAMPANIA: The most fertile plain of central Italy, which (I.ix.33) by means of viticulture made many rich men.

CARNUTES: Tribe of the Loire valley, considered by Caesar to live in the dead centre of Gaul; their territory was the heartland of the druidical religion in Gaul.

CARYSTUS: Town on the Greek island of Euboea, which (III.iii.14) produced a green-streaked marble.

CASTALIAN: The Castalian spring above *Delphi* (cf. *Pierus*) was thought to be a haunt of the Muses, and its waters believed to bring poetic inspiration.

CATULLUS: Roman poet (c. 84 –c. 54 B.C.) whose poem on the marriage of *Peleus* and *Thetis* contains an account of the desertion of Ariadne by *Theseus* (III.vi.41).

CERBERUS: Three-headed, three-tongued, snake-maned dog, who guarded the entrance to the underworld (III.iv.87).

CERES: Native Italian goddess of cereal crops, later identified with the Greek Demeter.

CERINTHUS: Lover of Sulpicia – see Introduction, p. 15.

CHARYBDIS: A whirlpool, opposite the cave of *Scylla*.

CHIAN: Wine from the Aegean island of Chios was one of the Romans' favourite vintages.

CHIMAERA: A mythical fire-breathing beast, lion in front, she-goat in the middle, and snake behind.

CHOASPES: River in Persia, called royal (III.vii.140ff.) because it was the only water the King of Persia was allowed to drink.

CICONES: Tribe who attacked *Ulysses* and his men after they had sacked the Cicones' chief city, Ismarus.

## Glossary

CILICIA: A loosely defined region of south-east Asia Minor, long before Tibullus' time claimed as a Roman province, but the scene of constant military activity against the mountain tribes.

CIMMERIAN: Traditionally the Cimmerians lived on the edge of the world in perpetual cold and dark; in their land was one of the entrances to the underworld, and the epithet became associated with the cold, dark regions of the underworld.

CIRCE: Archetypal witch, daughter of the sun-god, who in Homer's Odyssey turned men into wild animals with a magic potion.

COAN: See *Cos*.

CORNUTUS: See Introduction, p. 21.

COS: Aegean island, which produced in Roman times their most accessible supply of silk, particularly worn by courtesans etc., on account of its form-revealing thinness.

CRETAN: 'The Cretan girl' (III.vi.39) is Ariadne, daughter of *Minos*, deserted by *Theseus* on the island of Naxos, after he had carried her off from Crete as his bride.

'The Cretan' (III.vii.8) refers collectively to the humble but upright Cretans from Knossos selected by *Apollo* to perform the first sacrifice at his new temple at *Delphi*.

CUMAE: A town on the bay of Naples which produced good quality pottery (II.iii.52).

CUPID: The Latin 'cupido' simply means 'desire'; as a god Cupid was the Roman equivalent of Eros, who had collected in Hellenistic literature a symbolic apparatus of wings, bow and arrows, and sometimes firebrands, and was considered to be the son of *Venus*.

CYDNUS: River flowing to the sea near Tarsus in Syria.

CYNTHUS: One of the chief shrines of *Apollo*, who is sometimes referred to as 'Cynthius' (cf. *Diana*-Cynthia).

CYPRUS: Traditional haunt of Venus (III.iii.34).

DANAUS: Hero living in Egypt, whose fifty daughters, with the exception of the faithful Hypermnestra, were punished in the underworld by being set to fill water-pots with holes in for the crime of murdering on their wedding night their husbands, the fifty sons of King Aegyptus.

DELIA: See Introduction, pp. 21  31ff.

DELOS (DELIAN): Aegean island; birthplace and shrine of *Apollo* and *Diana*.

DELPHIC: Delphi, in central Greece, was the home of the most celebrated oracle of ancient times, inspired, it was thought, by *Apollo*, the god of prophecy.

DIANA: Roman goddess identified with the Greek Artemis; also identified with her were *Dictynna*, *Trivia*, and *Hecate*; goddess of hunting and wild animals, and chastity; associated also with the moon and magic.

DICTYNNA: Cretan goddess, alias Britomartis, later associated with *Diana*; hence she appears (I.iv.25) as goddess of hunting.

DIS: God of the underworld.

DOG-STAR, DOG-TIME: The dog-star is Sirius; the period of Sirius' greatest prominence in the night sky coincides in the Mediterranean area with hot, oppressive weather, and the star's influence was held responsible (III.vii.11). See *Icarus* for the legend of its origin.

DOMATOR: Chieftain of the *Iapydians* in the Illyrian war of 35–34 B.C.

ELIS, ELEAN: Olympia (I.iv.32), the home of the Olympic games, lay in the territory of Elis; one of the most prestigious events in the games was the chariot race, though it is unlikely that starting-gates were used there – these are a feature of professional chariot-racing in imperial Rome.

ELYSIAN FIELDS: In Greco-Roman myth, the part of the underworld set aside for the blessed; these include, for Tibullus, those who have died for love (I.iii.66), and wear the myrtle, sacred to Venus.

ERIGONE: See *Icarus*.

ETNA: Volcano in west Sicily, in legend the home of the Cyclops.

ETRURIA, ETRUSCAN: The civilization that preceded the Romans in Tuscany. Notable (III.iv.6) for developing the art of prophecy derived from a scrutiny of animals' entrails. III.v.1 may refer to any one of several hot-spring resorts in the area.

FALERNIAN: The Falernian plain was a fertile area of Campania, at the foot of Mt Massicus, which produced Rome's classic vintage wine.

FATHER, THE: See *Jupiter*.

GARONNE: River flowing north-west from the Pyrenees to the Bay of Biscay; the border of Roman *Aquitania*.

GAUL: Included not only France but some of Switzerland and the Low Countries.

GETAE: Originally a Thracian tribe, whose territory eventually shifted itself to the north of the Danube.

GUARDIAN-SPIRIT: See *Natalis*.

GYLIPPUS: Spartan general who contributed to the Athenian defeat in Sicily (413 B.C.).

GYNDES: The river of Babylon; while Cyrus was besieging the city, he lost his horse in the Gyndes, and spent the whole summer punishing the river by dividing it into 360 thigh-deep channels, thus giving the Babylonians time to recoup.

HAEMONIA: *Thessaly*; called after Mt Haemon.

HEBRUS: River of Eastern Thrace, into which area the kingdom of the *Getae* perhaps at one time stretched.

HECATE: An ancient Earth-goddess, associated with magic, the underworld, and also the moon, and worshipped at crossroads. Her common association with dogs (I.ii.54) perhaps arises from the effect of the moon on them.

HEROPHILE OF MARPESSUS: A *Sibyl* from Marpessus near *Troy*, who in one version of the *Aeneas* myth gave him a prophecy before he left for Italy.

IAPYDIA: District of north-west Yugoslavia, subdued by the future Augustus, with the help of *Messalla*, in 35 B.C.

ICARUS: (III.vii.12). This Icarus lived in Attica, entertained *Bacchus*, and was given the vine as a guest-present; he made some wine and gave it to his neighbours, who thought it poison and killed him; led by their dog, his daughter Erigone found the corpse and hanged herself. Icarus became the constellation Bootes, Erigone Virgo, and the dog Canicula, which includes the dog-star *Sirius*.

IDA: A mountain in *Phrygia*. See also *Ops*.

ILIA: Descendant of *Aeneas*, one of the Vestal virgins, mother by *Mars* of *Romulus and Remus*, the founders of Rome.

ILIUM: Troy.

INDIA: Generally conceived as the home of the jewels brought to

Rome by the eastern caravan route (II.ii.15); also a source of slaves (II.iii.59). III.viii.19 – The Romans seem to have freely confused the Red Sea, the Persian Gulf and the Indian Ocean.

ISIS: Egyptian goddess, whose Hellenized cult was very popular in the Roman world, especially among women. Some features of the cult are described I.iii.23ff. The 'sistrum' is a rattle; the painted tablets are thank-offerings hung up to commemorate a cure or other favour.

ITHACA: Small island at the mouth of the Corinthian gulf; home of *Ulysses*.

IXION: Punished in the underworld as described I.iii.73–4 for his attempted rape of *Juno*.

JOVE: English for *Jupiter*.

JUNO: Roman goddess, wife of Jupiter, known for her jealousy (II.iii.27). Also particularly the goddess of women, worshipped, like a man's Genius, by each individual as 'her own (particular) *Juno*'.

JUPITER: Chief and Father (I.iii.51, and I.iv.23) of the gods; god of the sky and weather, particularly of the thunderbolt. His overthrow of *Saturn* marked the end of the Golden Age of legend (I.iii.49). In Rome his temple was on the Capitoline Hill, of which the citadel was an outcrop (II.v.26).

KALENDS: The first day of the Roman month; see also *Mars*.

LAESTRYGONES: A tribe of cannibal giants in whose territory *Ulysses* landed. When he sent three men ahead to ask the way, they met a girl at the spring Artacie; she took them to her father, King Antiphates, who ate one of them; the tribe then destroyed all *Ulysses*' fleet except his own ship.

LARES: Spirits of the farmland, worshipped with the Penates at the 'lararium' or household shrine.

LAURENTUM, LAURENTINE: The 'laurens Ager' was in Latium on the left bank of the Tiber; here *Aeneas* first landed and founded his first settlement.

LAVINIUM: The second settlement founded by *Aeneas*, six miles from Laurentum.

LENAEUS: See *Bacchus*.

LETHE: River of the underworld whose waters brought forgetfulness.

## Glossary

LETO: Mother of the twins *Apollo* and *Diana*; also known as Latona.

LUCINA: Refers to *Diana*, though the name is more often used of *Juno* in her capacity of goddess of childbirth (III.iv.13).

LUNA: The moon, here associated with *Diana* (III.iv.2).

LYDIA: Kingdom of Croesus in north Asia Minor, in which was the gold-dust-carrying river Pactolus, the source of his fabulous wealth.

LYGDAMUS: See Introduction, p. 15.

MACER: See Introduction, p. 21.

MAGYNI: A Scythian tribe living around the river Don.

MARATHUS: See Introduction, p. 21.

MARCIAN WATER: Water from the Aqua Marcia, the coolest and most wholesome of the Roman aqueducts, built by Quintus Marcius Rex in 144 B.C. and repaired in Augustan times.

MARON: A priest who lived at Ismarus in the country of the *Cicones*. When *Ulysses* spared his life after sacking the city, Maron gave him a skin-bottle of very strong wine, which *Ulysses* later used to make the Cyclops drunk.

MARS: The Roman god of war; father by *Ilia* of *Romulus and Remus*, the founders of Rome. *Mars*' month (III.i.1) is March, the first day or *Kalends* of which was the feast of the Matronalia, when women received presents from their friends.

MEDEA: Princess of Colchis who eloped with Jason and the golden fleece, aided by the drugs and charms she had learnt; hence the archetype of a witch.

MELAMPUS: An archetypal prophet who learnt the future from bird-song etc.

MELES: River near Smyrna, one of the reputed birthplaces of Homer.

MEMPHIS: City in Egypt, centre of the worship of the bull-god Apis, who was represented in life by a carefully selected sacred bull, which, once dead, merged with the divinity of *Osiris*.

MESSALLA: See Introduction, pp. 10ff.

MESSALINUS: See Introduction, pp. 12, 13.

MINERVA: Goddess of crafts, especially spinning and weaving; like *Dictynna*, a virgin goddess and so not especially sympathetic to lovers (I.iv.26); she was very proud of her hair, having turned

Medusa's locks to snakes, simply because she compared them to Minerva's.

MINOS: King of Crete, father of Ariadne (see *Theseus*).

MOLORCHUS: The shepherd who gave Hercules shelter when he came to kill the Nemean lion.

MOPSOPUS: A mythical king of Attica, which was famous for its honey.

MUSES: Nine goddesses, who, under the leadership of *Apollo*, supplied the inspiration for the literary and musical arts. See also *Pierus*.

NATALIS: Personification of a man's birthday; closely linked to each man's Genius, or *guardian-spirit*, which he particularly worshipped on his birthday (cf. *Juno* for women).

NEAERA: See Introduction, pp. 21, 31ff.

NEMESIS: See Introduction, pp. 21, 31ff.

NEPTUNE: God of the sea; father of the Cyclops (III.vii.56).

NEREIDS: Sea-nymphs, daughters of Nereus, a sea-divinity.

NESTOR: Trojan war-hero noted for his wisdom, eloquence and longevity.

NISUS: In Greek legend the father of *Scylla*, who betrayed him to *Minos* by severing his lock of purple hair.

NUMICUS: Today a tiny stream which flows into the sea south of *Lavinium*; associated with the worship of *Vesta* and of the 'deus indiges' – 'the hero-god of the land'.

OLYMPUS: Sheer and frequently mist-shrouded mountain in northern Greece, thought to be the home of the gods.

OPS: Ops in Italian legend was the wife of Saturnus, but as Ops of *Ida* has become identified with the Phrygian Earth-mother-goddess Cybele, whose cult-image was carried round from city to city in chariots.

ORCUS: Name or title of *Dis*, the god of the underworld; hence (III. iii.37) the phrase 'the wealthy one', punning on the Latin word for rich.

OROATIS: River in Persia.

OSIRIS: Egyptian god, who in legend died and began a new life reigning in the underworld; a god of fertility, and so identified with the river Nile, and by the Romans with *Bacchus*; known also to many as a central figure in the ritual of his sister *Isis*, some of the details of which recur in his own worship.

PADAEAN: An Indian people living by the mouth of the Indus, and reputed to be cannibals; called neighbours of the sun-god from their extreme south-easterly position.

PALATINE: One of Rome's seven hills; one of the earliest to be settled.

PALES: Spirits of the flocks and herds (indiscriminately singular, plural, masculine, feminine). At their (his, her) festival, the Parilia the flocks were ritually purified for the coming year (I.i.36).

PALESTINIAN: Palestine was a district of the province of *Syria*; its white doves (I.vii.17) were birds dedicated to the eastern goddess Astarte.

PAN: Ancient Italian god, worshipped in connection with trees and woods, then as now equipped with his invention, the pan-pipes.

PANCHAIA: A supposed island in the Red Sea (see *India*), thought to produce a wealth of perfume-bearing plants.

PANNONIA: District of north Yugoslavia stretching to the Danube; partly conquered by the future Augustus with the help of *Messalla* (35–34 B.C.).

PELEUS: King of the Myrmidons in *Thessaly*; father of Achilles by the sea-nymph *Thetis*; their wedding was a favourite subject in art.

PELOPS: Son of *Tantalus*, who served up his children's flesh to the gods at a banquet. The truth was discovered and the children restored, but *Ceres* had eaten Pelops' shoulder and it had to be replaced with an ivory one.

PERSEPHONE: Wife of *Dis*, and so queen of the underworld. Her cult at Eleusis may be referred to in III.v.7–8; otherwise the 'praise-worthy goddess' is probably the *Bona Dea*.

PHAEACIA: The mythical island of Homer's Odyssey from which *Ulysses* was conveyed home to *Ithaca* at the end of his wanderings; later identified with Corcyra, modern Corfu, an important stage on the Romans' sea-route to Greece and the east.

PHOEBUS: See *Apollo*.

PHOLOE: See Introduction, p. 21.

PHRYGIA: I.iv.70 – 'Phrygian music'; Phrygia was the home of the worship of Cybele, whose adepts had slashed off their privates in a frenzied religious dance-ritual. Otherwise, as at II.i.86, Phrygian music is simply music for the flute or pipe, thought to have originated there. III.iii.13 – Phrygian marble was a white marble quarried at Synnas.

PHRYNE: Nemesis' go-between – see Introduction, pp. 32–3.

PHYTO: *Sibyl* of Samos.

PIERUS, PIERIAN, PIERIDES: Pierus was a king of Thessaly whose nine daughters bore the names of the nine *Muses*. The patronymic 'Pierid' thus comes to mean a *Muse*. There was also a mountain in *Thessaly* which got the name Pierus, probably being considered, like Mts Helicon and Parnassus, to be one of the *Muses*' haunts.

PLUTO: Another name for *Dis*, the god of the underworld.

PRAISEWORTHY GODDESS: See under *Persephone* and *Bona Dea*.

PRIAPUS: God of fertility, denoted by a large phallus; also of gardens, in which his statue, armed with a billhook, acted as part scarecrow, and part guardian spirit; reckoned to be the son of *Bacchus*.

PYLOS: Home of *Nestor* in the western Peloponnese.

ROMULUS AND REMUS: The twin sons of *Ilia* and *Mars*, suckled by a she-wolf; actual founders of Rome on the seven hills. Romulus later quarrelled with Remus and killed him.

RUTULIANS: Indigenous Italian tribe who under their leader *Turnus* were opposed to Aeneas and his men settling in Italy.

SAINTONGE: The coastal district just north of the *Garonne* estuary, which derives its name from the Gallic tribe the Santones.

SAMIAN: Samos in the Aegean produced (II.iii.51) a type of inexpensive but good-quality pottery.

SATURN: The father of *Jupiter*, identified with the Greek Cronos. I.iii.18 – Saturn's day is the modern Saturday, and the Jewish Sabbath, on which no work or travel was permitted.
I.iii.35 – The age of Saturn was when Saturn ruled the gods and men, before he was overthrown by Jupiter; in Roman myth, the golden age of the noble savage.
III.iii.33 – Saturn's daughter is *Juno*.

SCYLLA: Sea-monster living in a cave opposite *Charybdis*, and feeding on the flesh of captured sailors.

SCYTHIA: Roughly, all the country north of the Danube and the Black Sea, whose inhabitants were in Roman times a byword for barbarity.

SEMELE: Mother of *Bacchus*, by *Jupiter*.

SERVIUS: See Introduction, p. 8.

SIBYL: The name given to trance-prophetesses in various shrines. II.v.15 and 19 must refer to the Sibyl of Cumae, as in Virgil's Aeneid. See ll.65ff. for other Sibyls, e.g. of *Tibur* (l.69). It is possible that they were all conceived of as manifestations of a single being. The trance was perhaps partly induced by the chewing of bay-leaves (see l.63), and virginity was an essential qualification. See Introduction for the Sibylline books, pp. 39–40.

SIDON: Like *Tyre* Sidon had a flourishing trade in the purple dye extracted from the murex shell-fish, and in cloth dyed with it.

SIRENS: Beautiful creatures who lured sailors to their deaths on the shores of their rocky island with their lovely singing.

SIRIUS: See *Dog-star*.

STYGIAN: Styx was the river of the underworld first encountered by the newly dead, who were ferried across it, one way only, by the ferryman Charon.

SYRIAN: Because of the transit trade from further east, Syria was conceived as the home of perfumes and spices, often produced (III.iv.28) by plants exuding dew-like droplets.

SYRTIS: Collectively the 'Syrtes' are the shallow waters between Tunisia and Cyrenaica, which acquired an exaggerated reputation for dangerousness.

TAENARUS: In Laconia in the Peloponnese; source of a much-prized marble.

TAMYRIS: Queen of the Massagetae, a tribe living to the east of Armenia, who, when threatened with invasion by Cyrus, warned him not to cross the River Araxes. He did and was killed in the ensuing battle.

TANAIS: River flowing south-west into the Black Sea; modern Don.

TANTALUS: For his crime, see *Pelops*. He was punished in the under-world as described in I.iii.77.

TAURUS: The Taurus mountain range in south-east Asia Minor, whose tribes long resisted Roman annexation.

THEBAN: III.vi.24 – The Theban mother is Agave, who, while cele-brating a Bacchic ritual in the mountains, tore apart, under the influence of the god, the body of her own son Pentheus, who had come to spy on her.

THERA: Aegean island, from which (III.vii.139) Cyrene in north Africa was colonized.

THESEUS: King of Athens, who abandoned his bride Ariadne on the island of Naxos.

THESSALY: The north-eastern part of the Greek peninsula, tradition-ally a land of magic and witches.

THETIS: A sea-nymph, who was married to *Peleus*.

TIBUR: II.v.69 – The Sibyl of Tibur near Rome, who was called Albunea, was subsequently worshipped as a divinity near the falls of the *Anio*, through which river she was supposed to have swum without wetting the prophetic scrolls she was carrying to Rome.

TISIPHONE: The chief of the Furies, set over damned spirits to torture them.

TITAN: III.vii.50, 113, 156 – Titan here is the sun-god, whose daily course is the measure of time.

TITIUS: See Introduction, p. 21.

TITYOS: Punished in the underworld as described (I.iii.75) for his attempted rape of *Leto*.

TRIVIA: Goddess of the cross-roads, sites always associated with magic and the darker powers; identified with *Diana*.

TROY: Home town of the Greeks' enemy in the Trojan war; original home of *Aeneas* and his men.

TURNUS: Prince of the *Rutulians*, eventually killed in single combat by *Aeneas*.

TUSCULUM: Town fifteen miles south-east of Rome, just off the part of the Via Flaminia that *Messalla* repaired.

TYRE, TYRIAN: Phoenician town; built on an island; hence its tall buildings (I.vii.19); home of the manufacture of the best-quality purple dye in the ancient world; hence 'Tyrian' refers (I.ix.70) to stuffs dyed with this product.

ULYSSES: Trojan-war-hero, noted for cunning, and the adventures he had in the ten years it took him to get home from *Troy* to *Ithaca*.

VALGIUS: See Introduction, p. 21.

VELABRUM: Flat marshy ground between the Capitoline, Palatine, and Aventine hills of Rome; still, in the classical period, liable to flooding by the Tiber.

VENUS: Roman goddess of sexual love; identified with Greek Aphrodite and hence like her thought to have been born from the severed genitals of Uranus as they fell into the sea (I.ii.41–2); mother of *Cupid*, and also, by Anchises, of *Aeneas*, founder of Rome.

VERTUMNUS: Etruscan god, whose origins were obscure even to the Romans; but an ability to change to suit circumstances was popularly attributed to him.

VESTA: Goddess of the hearth, in whose temple in Rome an undying fire was tended by the Vestal virgins.

VULCAN: The Roman god of fire, forging and volcanoes.

# MORE ABOUT PENGUINS

*Penguinews*, which appears every month, contains details of all the new books issued by Penguins as they are published. From time to time it is supplemented by *Penguins in Print*, which is a complete list of all available books published by Penguins. (There are well over three thousand of these.)

A specimen copy of *Penguinews* will be sent to you free on request, and you can become a subscriber for the price of the postage. For a year's issues (including the complete lists) please send 30p if you live in the United Kingdom, or 60p if you live elsewhere. Just write to Dept EP, Penguin Books Ltd, Harmondsworth, Middlesex, enclosing a cheque or postal order, and your name will be added to the mailing list.

Note: *Penguinews* and *Penguins in Print* are not available in the U.S.A. or Canada

# THE POEMS OF PROPERTIUS

*Translated by A. E. Watts*

Sextus Propertius (c. 50–c. 10 B.C.) wrote during the Augustan period. Most of his poems, which show a superb mastery of the elegiac couplet, were inspired by his mistress, Cynthia, whom he idealized (at any rate in his first book) with an infectious spontaneity. As the affair degenerated into faithlessness and quarrels, Propertius began to find his subjects in contemporary events and manners, in history and legend. But it is his love poetry, with its many delightful vignettes of life in Rome, which ensure for him a unique, if not a major position in Latin literature.

# THE LAST POETS OF
# IMPERIAL ROME

*Translated by Harold Isbell*

This is a collection of Latin verse, translated into English, of the second to fifth centuries A.D. from all parts of the Roman Empire and beyond: Italy, Spain, Carthage, Gaul, Ireland. There is a wide variety of themes: pastoral, mythological, Christian, philosophical, aristocratic life and customs, the sacking of Rome by the Visigoths and regrets at the passing of the Empire. Running through all this is the theme of the fall of Rome, both literally in the destruction of the city, and generally in its gradual decline as cultural and political world centre.

Amongst the various poems included are *The Moselle* by Ausonius, *Hymns for the Various Hours and Days* by Prudentius and the anonymous *The Night Watch of Venus*.

# CLASSICS FROM THE AGE OF CICERO

## CICERO
### On the Good Life

His tentative and undogmatic reflections on the good life, in which he discusses duty, friendship, the training of a statesman, and the importance of moral integrity in the search for happiness. *Translated by Michael Grant.*

## CATULLUS
### The Poems of Catullus

The great lyrical poet here recorded the love he felt for the Lesbia who is the subject of many of the poems. They also reveal his urbane and worldly-wise wit, and his genius for natural description. *Translated by Peter Whigham*

## LUCRETIUS
### On the Nature of the Universe

Lucretius wrote with the force of an unshakeable personal conviction in the materialism of Epicurus. His work is an appeal to a disillusioned age to take comfort from the sanity of science. *Translated by Ronald Latham*

*also available*

## CICERO
Selected Works *and* Selected Political Speeches
*Translated by Michael Grant*

## SALLUST
Jugurthine War/Conspiracy of Catiline
*Translated by S. A. Handford*

## CAESAR
The Civil War *Translated by Jane F. Mitchell*
The Conquest of Gaul *Translated by S. A. Handford*

# THE PENGUIN CLASSICS

*Some Recent Volumes*

**PHILIPPE DE COMMYNES**
Memoirs   *Michael Jones*

**BEOWULF**
*Michael Alexander*

**SIX YUAN PLAYS**
*Liu Jung-en*

**CERVANTES**
Exemplary Stories   *C. A. Jones*

**BALZAC**
A Murky Business   *Herbert J. Hunt*

**CICERO**
On the Nature of the Gods   *Horace C. P. McGregor*

**ZOLA**
Nana   *George Holden*

**VIRGIL**
The Pastoral Poems   *E. V. Rieu*

**EURIPIDES**
Orestes and Other Plays   *Philip Vellacott*

**BOCCACCIO**
The Decameron   *G. H. McWilliam*